Any Sunrise

Luna Family Trilogy, Volume 2

Kimberly R. Rose

Published by Kimberly R. Rose, 2023.

Paperback ISBN: 979-8-9882242-3-5
    Ebook ISBN: 979-8-9882242-2-8

First edition: August 1st, 2023

Written by Kimberly R. Rose
    Cover illustration by C. J.'s Art & Design

Table of Contents

To my fellow spoonies out there - this one is for all of you.

Chapter 1

"Look Drew!" Alexica called to her twin brother. "Look how high I climbed!" The wind blew her hair into her face as she sat down on a tree branch, keeping careful hold on another branch in front of her.

"That's not that high!" Drew called back from his position a little lower on the tree. "I can get up there, just not as fast as you."

Lexi shrugged, letting herself relax as she glanced around the crowded backyard. It was the neighborhood's annual block party. "There's a lot of people here." She noted, letting go of the tree with one of her hands. She felt herself slip, and frantically reached for the branch but her fingers came up empty. The last thing Lexi remembered was hearing her older sister's frantic scream.

*** Fourteen years later ***

Lexi tried to breathe, but she found that harder and harder to do through the tears. *Try to calm down. You need to calm down.* She wound her arms around her waist in an attempt to comfort herself. *Breathe Lexi, just breathe. That's all you need to do right now.* She felt a soft head on her knee, and she reached one hand down to pet her dog.

She did that for a couple minutes. Just sat in her wheelchair and focused on her breathing while she petted Daisy. She closed her eyes and tried not to let any more tears come. They were just making it harder for her to breathe. When she finally got a bit of control, she reached for her water bottle and took a sip. The cool water soothing her after the tears. She used her fingers to wipe the tears off her cheeks and tried to ignore the pain that came with every breath she took. That was normal, especially after all she'd done today.

"Accomplished," Lexi whispered, trying to remind herself. "All I accomplished today."

But her mind couldn't help but focus on the fact that a twenty-three-year-old like her should be able to accomplish a lot more in a day. Her twin brother had accomplished an entire day of teaching

1

school, then probably gone to his own home and made himself dinner and who knew after that.

What had she accomplished today? Laundry and dinner. Just her small load of laundry in the morning, and dinner tonight. She hadn't even been able to help her parents with the dishes as she normally did. Hher body was too tired and heavy to move.

Lexi tried not to think about her plans for tomorrow, and how they may be canceled now. She may have done enough to make tomorrow very painful for herself. Daisy nudged her knee, sensing that her owner needed more comforting. Lexi began to pet her again.

With her chronic illness pain was a normal part of her life. Ever since she'd fallen out of a tree when she was nine, it had been central to her life.

Her body didn't work like a normal person's body did. Her autonomic nervous system didn't work correctly; meaning her heart rate, blood pressure, breathing and digestion were affected and were often unpredictable.

Some moments, like now, it took conscious thought for her to breathe normally. It was something that happened to her often, so she didn't panic or worry about it. It just took her a little while to calm herself and regulate her body a little better.

"Lexi, I'm going to bed. Let me know if you need anything. You know my phone is always on," Her mother - Connie - called from the other side of Lexi's closed bedroom door.

"Okay Mom," Lexi replied, trying not to let more tears come to her eyes. Daisy was a trained service dog, and could go get things for Lexi or carry them for her if she needed. She could alert Lexi to her blood pressure or heart rate extremes. Some moments though, Lexi just wanted her mom.

Lexi had never had a boyfriend or really gone out on dates. She'd wanted to when she was younger, but quickly found she was too high-maintenance for many men. She dreamed of finding the perfect man, one who would be by her side no matter her health. That man – she was convinced – existed only in her dreams. Daisy gave her someone besides herself to take care of and love.

She longed for a paid job, but that hadn't happened yet. Her therapist had told her there was a job out there she could do, but so far, she'd only found volunteer opportunities. Her health was unpredictable, she could be fine one moment them close to fainting the next. It made her very unreliable, and most jobs weren't flexible. She also had an intolerance to both heat and cold. Any environment she worked in or stayed for a while had to be the perfect temperature.

Trying to find out what that job could be was taking a lot more years than Lexi would have liked. Right now, her parents still paid for everything - her food, clothing, personal items, Daisy's food and vet bills – sinceshe didn't have any money of her own. She suspected that Drew was contributing to that fund but he refused to admit that.

Lexi carefully stood up, glad to find she wasn't too dizzy at the moment. It was coming - she was sure - but at least she had time to get ready for bed. She moved as quickly as she could without making herself too tired. She got dressed, took her last pill of the day, and brushed her teeth. She moved her wheelchair to her bedroom door and made sure her cane was next to her bed, then turned off her main bedroom lights. Relief washed over her that she'd made it through her nightly routine. She was okay, all she needed to was sleep.

The room was now lit with Christmas lights her dad had strung up her ceiling years ago, attached to a wireless outlet so she could turn them on and off from her phone. For the days she couldn't get out of bed it was helpful to be able to turn them on and off herself. Daisy could turn on the bedroom lights for her if she needed, but they were brighter than the Christmas lights.

Lexi looked at her phone screen, noting a text from Drew. *Natala will be at dinner tomorrow night?* She checked the time the text had been sent, realizing it was over an hour ago.

Lexi was terrible at checking her phone. It wasn't a habit, and sometimes the screen made her head hurt when she looked at it too long. Technology in general wasn't her favorite thing either.

She smiled as she read Drew's text again, quickly typing back. *Apparently, I didn't know anything about it until a couple hours ago when Mom told me. I think Mom has known for a while though. I'm supposed to take it easy at chess tomorrow so I'm able to function at dinner.*

Drew's reply came quickly. *Any indication about why she's coming? I don't think she has visited for a year now, last time she came and only stayed for two days. She couldn't even make it back for Christmas.*

Lexi read that text, then bit her lip. *Has it really been that long?* It was hard to keep track. Her older sister had moved away when she was eighteen and the visits had always been sporadic. Natala missing Christmas this year had been noticed though, especially since Natala's birthday was on Christmas. It had been weird for Christmas to just be about Christmas and not Natala's birthday. *I don't know anything. Maybe she got engaged?* A bit of jealousy washed over her at that thought.

A moment after she sent that message, her phone began to ring. "What?" She answered as she lay back on her bed.

"Natala broke up with Nolen, did Mom not tell you that?" Drew asked her, seeming surprised.

Lexi sat back up again, then frowned and winced as pain went through her head. She shouldn't have done that. "What?" She asked weakly as she tried to blink away the blackness.

"Lexi, don't hurt yourself."

She sighed, the blackness leaving her vision. "I sat up too fast, I'm fine." She wished that Drew didn't know her as well as he did. How could he pick up when she'd done something just from her voice? It wasn't like spending nine months together in their mother's womb had made them telepathic.

"Did you really not know that Natala broke it off? That was back in May or something that she called Mom and told her."

"I really didn't know. Mom doesn't tell me a whole lot; thinks she's protecting me." Lexi didn't have to voice her thoughts on that for her brother, he knew exactly how it made her feel. She loved her mother very much, but some moments she resented the fact that she needed her mom's help. It was a problem that came with being disabled, with having chronic health issues.

"I thought they were a moment away from getting engaged. Her relationship lasted way longer than any of yours have."

"Very funny." There was a crash in the background as Drew spoke. "Um, I got to go. My new foster just knocked down my glass of soda and he's about to drink it. Oh, and I need to talk to you tomorrow. I have a coworker you need to meet." Before there was a chance to reply, the phone started beeping in her ear as the call ended.

Lexi plugged her phone into her nightstand as she felt a smile come to her face for the first time that day. Drew had a soft heart. One of his exes had convinced him he would be a perfect pet foster parent. It probably had a large part to do with her being the foster coordinator at their local animal shelter. The girl hadn't stuck; but the fostering had. Some of the animals Drew ended up with had big personalities.

"So much different than you Daisy." She told the golden retriever, who wagged her tail. "You are a perfect angel, yes you are." She scratched Daisy behind her ears.

So, Natala is single. Lexi stood up and pulled back the covers on her bed as she considered that fact.

Her older sister had always been a hero of sorts to her. She'd managed to do everything Lexi could only dream of doing. Natala had moved out and a state away soon after she graduated high school. She'd been working since she was sixteen, bought a car when she turned eighteen. She'd met her boyfriend in high school and had followed him out of state. That was something Lexi envied. She wished there was a man who loved her enough to follow her if she moved.

Except now that relationship was over. Lexi wondered if her sister was okay, if the breakup had been hard. The sisters had never been close, she had admired Natala from afar. If jealousy was considered a form of admiration. They hadn't spoken outside of Natala's visits since she'd moved.

"Your normal is different from other people's normal," Lexi reminded herself as she climbed into the bed. One of her therapist's favorite sayings; one that she tried to appreciate. It was harder and harder because the older she got, the more she wished she could be normal.

Lexi took a deep breath in, then let it out. She needed sleep right now. Maybe her questions would be answered at dinner. She used her phone to turn off the lights, then opened her music app and began to listen to music through her sleep headphones.

Chapter 2

Lexi found herself cleaning up as quickly as she could after the chess club the next day. It wasn't as quickly as everyone else, but that was her normal. Held at the local library, the chess club was an afterschool activity. Kids could come and learn how to play chess or just practice. It had been a club Lexi had joined when she was eleven and looking for a hobby.

Chess had been a hobby she could do easily most days. It was sitting down and playing a game. It took more mental strength than physical strength, and Lexi definitely had more of that. When she'd aged out of the club, she'd elected to become one of the volunteers. It gave her something productive to do and she enjoyed playing chess and teaching the game to kids and teens.

"Thanks for your help, Lexi. Maybe you should take a nap when you get home; you seem a little tired today," Patsy - the librarian who had started the chess club - told her.

Lexi gave Patsy a small smile as she put a rook into the bag of pieces. "I did a bit too much yesterday. I'm trying not to overdo it today," She explained, adding the last pawn to the bag before she pulled the drawstrings closed. Her body was already warning her that she should take a nap, but she was too excited to do that even if she'd had time. Natala was coming to dinner.

"If it's too much, you don't have to come every time," Patsy told her as she gathered chess boards from around the tables.

Lexi tossed the bag into the box with the other chess pieces and wheeled away from the table. "I don't want to miss this; I love the chess club. And I like my routines. Chess club is part of my normal Tuesday." She glanced at her watch and blinked.

"I need to get going!" She exclaimed, realizing it was later than she'd thought. "My sister is coming for dinner tonight. I'll see you on Thursday."

7

"See you Thursday!" Patsy called back as Lexi whistled for Daisy. Once the dog had joined her, she wheeled out of the room. She got onto the elevator after Daisy and pushed the button for the main floor, then pulled out her phone to make sure she hadn't missed anything. "Nope," she said aloud as she swiped away the notification reminder her mom had set up for dinner.

Daisy came trotting over and followed her owner onto the elevator. The pair rode the elevator to the main floor as Lexi checked her phone to make sure she hadn't missed any messages. *All good*, she confirmed as the elevator doors opened.

Tossing her phone on her lap, she wheeled herself out to the parking lot. She unlocked her car. *Technically my parent's car*, she reminded herself as she clicked the button on her key fob to unlock the doors.

Grabbing the driver's door handle and using it to help herself stand up, she opened the back door. "In Daisy," she instructed, then carefully folded up her wheelchair and put it beside the dog. She slid into the driver's seat and locked all the car doors.

Lexi could walk just fine, there was nothing wrong with her legs specifically. She'd been using a wheelchair and occasionally a cane since she was ten. By now she was used to the weird looks she got from people when they saw her stand up and walk. Walking just was something that took her energy away quickly, and the wheelchair helped a lot with that.

Lexi started the car, noting gladly that she wouldn't be late for dinner. "Off we go, Daisy," she said as she pulled out of the parking spot. Similar to walking, Lexi could drive. It wasn't something she could do for long periods of time and on certain days she was too tired, but she was very glad she could drive at least to chess club twice a week.

"It would be embarrassing to sit outside and wait for my mom to pick me up," Lexi spoke her thoughts aloud, then frowned. "Or maybe not embarrassing. I'm not sure what the right word is, but it is a lot nicer to be able to drive myself. And you Daisy, you like rides in the car, don't you?"

Of course, it also helped a lot that the library was five blocks from their house, she acknowledged. As children, Lexi and her siblings had often walked there.

Lexi pulled into her driveway and parked beside the garage, then got out of the car. She got out her wheelchair, let Daisy out, and wheeled her way through the garage into the house. They had a front door, but the front door did not have a ramp. So, Lexi had to go through the garage when she was using her wheelchair.

"How was chess?" Connie called as Lexi wheeled into the kitchen. Lexi undid Daisy's halter and vest, then told the dog to go lay down in her bed.

"The same as always," Lexi shrugged as she opened the fridge and pulled out a bottle of water. "Nothing crazy happened, no new kids or anything." She opened the water bottle and added a packet of electrolytes, then put the lid back on it and shook it up. "When is Natala getting here?" She asked as she watched her mom chop up carrots.

Connie glanced over to the clock on the oven. "An hour or so, I didn't get an exact time. I'm not sure if she is coming straight from Illinois or if she's been in Wisconsin."

Lexi took a sip of her water. "I'm assuming Drew will be here as soon as school is over?"

"Hopefully. I need him to grill the burgers. Your father is working late tonight, he had a meeting or something. I'm not sure when he will be home." Connie opened the fridge and pulled out the celery. "Can you shred some lettuce for me? I'm making a seven-layer salad."

Lexi wheeled over to the table and set down her water bottle, noting the lettuce and glass dish were already there instead of on the counter. Her mom had intended for her to do this, or she'd have left it on the counter where Lexi couldn't reach. "I was wondering what carrots had to do with hamburgers," Lexi called as she slowly stood up, and walked over to the sink to wash her hands.

"I know that it's September. Technically it is fall, but it still seems like summer. Hamburgers and seven-layer salad seem like the perfect summer food," Connie explained as she started chopping celery.

Lexi sat back down in her wheelchair and began to rip the lettuce into smaller leaves for the first layer of the salad. She heard a car door. "Drew must be here."

"Sounds like it," Connie agreed, walking over to the door and opening it for her son.

Lexi finished ripping the lettuce into shreds as Drew walked into the house. "Home sweet home," He said as he set his bag down on the floor. Before he could say anything else, Daisy had run over to him for petting.

"You're acting like a child!" Connie pretended to scold him. "Your bag doesn't belong on the floor, and where is my hug?"

Drew rolled his eyes at Lexi as he petted Daisy. Lexi put her hand over her mouth to hide her laughter.

"I heard that," Connie told her with a stern glance, only making Lexi laugh more.

"So, why is Natala coming?" Drew asked as he opened the fridge and pulled out a can of root beer. "Daisy, I'm not going to share with you," he told the dog as she tried to lick the can. "You can go lay down."

"Why?" Connie sighed as she took the glass dish from Lexi and brought it to the counter, then added the carrots and the celery. "My eldest daughter is coming home to see me and the two of you want to know why?"

Drew and Lexi shared a glance, silently wondering why their mother was so dramatic. Lexi nodded out to the patio, then at the hamburgers and raised her eyebrows.

Drew frowned and looked around the house, then gave Lexi a questioning glance.

Lexi gave a tiny shrug of her shoulders and mouthed the word "meeting" as their mother turned to see what they were doing.

"Out loud, you both know how to talk," Connie reminded them. She grabbed the hamburgers and set them in Drew's hands. "Please grill these, since your father is working late."

"Told you." Lexi whispered with a grin as Drew walked out onto the patio.

"I carried the two of you for nine months, only for you to have conversations behind my back." Connie shook her head as she pulled out a bag of cheese. She tried to look upset but Lexi could see the smile she was trying to hide.

Lexi sat back in her wheelchair and watched her mom move around the kitchen. "Mom, why aren't you asking Drew about his day? You asked me about chess. He worked so hard teaching all those children."

"I've been teaching children my entire life." Drew told her as he carried the tray now devoid of hamburgers into the house. He picked up a pair of tongs as he raised his eyebrows at Lexi. "That's you, you were the child I taught."

Lexi glared at her twin brother. "Says the one who is two minutes younger," she said pointedly.

Connie cleared her throat, causing the twins to look at her. "I don't know how the two of you always seem to revert to acting like children when you are together. It must be a twin thing. I think your sister is here."

The latter of the sentences was delivered casually, but made Lexi and Drew share a glance. This visit seemed out of the ordinary. It wasn't a normal time of year for Natala to visit. Most of her visits happened over a weekend.

Today was a Tuesday, and Natala would have had to take off work to come home. Drew frowned, looking at Lexi for answers. She widened her eyes and lifted her shoulders in a shrug as Connie ran out to greet her daughter.

"Don't forget to ask me about Birdie before I leave," Drew said as they heard footsteps and voices coming from the garage.

Lexi frowned. What was Birdie? An animal, perhaps Drew's latest foster?

She quickly forgot about that when her mother and sister walked into the house with a unfamiliar man following them.

"Lexi, Drew, this is Tony." Natala introduced when she spotted her younger siblings. "Tony, these are my younger siblings. This is Lexi and this is Drew."

Drew nodded at Tony, then gave Lexi a questioning glance before he stepped back out to the patio to continue grilling. Lexi didn't have any answers for him, she wasn't sure herself. After all, she'd just found out Natala was no longer dating Nolen last night. "Nice to meet you," she said to the man.

Had her sister really met another man already? An unexpected pang of jealousy hit Lexi. Her sister had all the luck it seemed. But her sister was an able-bodied, hard-working sort of girl; something Lexi could never be. It made sense Natala was more attractive to the male species.

"It is wonderful to meet you as well, Natala has talked a lot about all of you." Lexi was surprised to hear the man had an accent. She couldn't place where it was from, somewhere in Europe perhaps?

Lexi glanced at her mom, wondering if she had known that Natala was bringing someone tonight. She couldn't tell, her mom was rushing around the kitchen trying to prepare things the same she would any other day.

"Natala, please set the table. Lexi, pull the chair in from the living room." Connie relayed.

Lexi wheeled over to the living room. That was her answer. Her mom would have already had the chair at the table if she'd known Natala wasn't coming alone.

"I've got it." Tony said, picking up the chair before Lexi could reach it. "Where does it go?"

"At the end of the table please," Lexi replied as she followed him. "Where are you from?" She asked. "Your accent is lovely."

Tony chuckled and glanced over at Natala. "Thank you. I was born in Italy, but grew up in the States. I work as an international photographer so I suppose I pick up a bit of many accents."

"Unless he gets passionate about something," Natala laughed as she and Tony shared a secret smile. "Then you can really hear the Italian." She set the plates around the table, then glanced at her mom. "What do we need for silverware?"

Connie waved her hand. "Forks should do it. Why don't you add bowls for the salad in case someone wants them? Maybe in the center of the table so they don't get wasted."

Lexi wheeled carefully around her sister and pulled a potholder out of a drawer. She pulled condiments and cheese out of the fridge, setting each in her lap. After using her foot to close the fridge door, she wheeled over to the table.

"You can take less trips using that," Tony observed.

Lexi laughed as he set the condiments on the table beside the hot pad. "I've never really thought about that, but I guess so. It probably takes the same amount of time as it would anyone else taking two trips."

Tony shrugged. "No lost efficiency there." He looked at Natala as she set the forks on the table. "Is there anything I can do to help?"

"I think that's about covered now; we are just waiting on Drew to finish with the grill," Connie told him with a smile. "Why don't you just take a seat, and Natala can finish putting the dishes on the table. I need to make a quick call." She excused herself and walked down the hall.

Natala frowned and looked at Lexi. "What is she doing?"

"Calling Dad," Lexi explained as she took the dish Natala set on her lap and wheeled it to the table. "He had to work late or had a meeting, I'm not altogether sure. But she wants to find out how late he will be."

Natala sat down on a chair beside the one Tony had taken. "That's odd."

Lexi met Drew's gaze through the screen door. It wasn't that odd for their father to be working late. It was something he'd done more and more as the business grew. Of course, Natala had moved seven years ago, so she wouldn't have realized.

"Business is booming." Lexi replied noncommittally.

"Alexica, Natala told me a bit about your POTS, but she neglected to mention you have an adorable helper. What's her name?" Tony asked as Daisy stood beside the sliding door watching Drew.

Lexi laughed. "Her name is Daisy. She is the best helper I've ever had." She glanced at her brother. "Drew was the one who encouraged our parents to get her for me, because he wasn't going to be able to help me all the time for the rest of our lives."

Tony shrugged. "Seems like you could use his help to your advantage, even with Daisy. What does she do to help you?"

"She alerts me to my flares before I see them, for one," Lexi gave the dog a loving glance. "She will paw me or bark at me or jump on my lap if I'm in my wheelchair. Whatever it takes to get me to realize I need to check my blood pressure. And then I can take steps to fix it, whether it is high or low."

"Daisy retrieves things for Lexi too," Natala inserted. "That's the part I've always been jealous of. Lexi just has to ask Daisy to get her a water bottle and that smart little dog can open the fridge and get her a cold bottle of water."

"My own little butler," Lexi agreed. Of course, all the times she used that particular skill of Daisy's were when she couldn't move enough to get water for herself.

Drew brought the finished burgers into the house at the same time her mom walked back into the kitchen.

"Your dad should be here in an hour; we will just go ahead and save him a plate," Connie replied with a smile. "He is training a new mechanic this week, and it has been a lot of late nights."

Lexi and Drew frowned in unison; it was only Tuesday. Lexi remembered her dad being home at a normal time last night, so maybe her mom meant the rest of the week would be late nights.

She shrugged it off. "Mom, do you want to pray?" She asked, trying to move this dinner along.

After Connie blessed the food, the family started to eat. "So, Natala, how did you meet Tony?" Drew asked as he stabbed a hamburger with his fork.

Natala blushed as she spooned some peaches onto her plate. "We met on a flight to Italy," she admitted.

Lexi's eyes widened as she looked at her sister. "You went to Italy?" She asked in shock. "Like Italy the country or is there a city called Italy in the States that you are speaking about?"

Natala laughed, covering her mouth with her hand. "I should see if that is a city in the States, I'm not sure. I went to the country of Italy, it's a beautiful place with beautiful sunsets." She and Tony locked eyes for a moment and seemed to forget the others were there.

"Well." Connie blinked as she looked at her oldest. "You didn't tell us you were going to Italy."

Natala blushed again, this time looking embarrassed. "It was just something I needed to do; I didn't know that then but I did."

Lexi silently wondered how one could spend unimaginable amounts of money to leave the country and claim it as a need. Then again, Natala actually had a job and made her own money so it was a lot more affordable to her. It helped that there were no health restrictions for her older sister to consider.

"What was the best part of Italy?" Drew asked before taking a bite of his burger.

Natala finished her bite of peach before she answered. "The gelato," she sighed. "It's magical, and so much better in Italy, but the stuff here is pretty good too if you get it from the right place."

Lexi took a bite of the seven-layer salad and tried to imagine Italy. It was probably pretty; she'd give it that. The food had always sounded divine there. But her body wouldn't be able to function well. There was so much she would have to take with her, just in case any number of things happened. Not that a flight was even a consideration; she'd been heavily warned against them.

"So, what are you doing in Wisconsin this week?" Drew asked Natala. Lexi silently applauded him for asking the question that had been on both their minds all day.

Natala smiled. "I have a couple job interviews."

"You're moving home?" Connie asked, her fork halfway to her mouth. "Is my baby moving home?"

Natala shrugged. "I'm working on it. I still have to actually find a job and a place to live, but that's the plan."

"My baby's moving home!" Connie got up from her chair and walked over to hug Natala.

"I thought I was your baby," Drew reminded his mother, who ignored him.

"You can live here of course; your bedroom is ready and waiting. I turned Drew's into a guest bedroom a while ago but yours is just as you left it."

"So much for being the baby," Lexi told her brother with a laugh, trying not to think about her own bedroom.

It went without saying that it was exactly as she'd left it as well - that morning. She'd never moved out or given her mom the opportunity to change her room into something else.

***

Later that evening - after her dad had arrived home and the family had spoken all about Natala's move - Lexi wheeled herself out onto the porch.

She was getting over-simulated by all the people talking at once. And she was a bit overwhelmed at the thought of her older sister moving back into the house. It had been just her and her parents for a year now, and she enjoyed the quiet.

Daisy joined her, lying beside her chair with a sigh. It seemed she'd had enough of the people too.

"Too much noise?" Her brother asked.

Lexi smiled as Drew sat down beside her on the porch, effectively making himself a lot shorter as she had her chair and he was sitting on the floor.

"Yeah," She admitted, glancing behind herself into the house. "I'm glad Mom and Dad are happy."

Drew shrugged. "Tony seems good for her. Nolen never came when she visited."

Lexi frowned, trying to remember the last time that she'd seen her sister's ex. She couldn't remember either way. "Really? Never?"

"Not that I can remember. He was born and raised here so obviously we met him. Once they moved, I don't think he ever came back. His parents moved away like a couple months after he and Natala did."

"Interesting." Lexi tried to file that away in her memory.

Tony did seem nice, and Natala certainly seemed to like him. They couldn't keep their eyes off each other, something that had stood out to her. Lexi was jealous, she'd be the first to admit it. Natala may have found her soulmate. She should be happy for her sister, and she was. But the jealousy was there too.

"You had something you wanted to talk to me about?" She reminded her twin softly.

"Oh yeah, Birdie," Drew was quiet for a moment. "You know that spreadsheet graph book thing you made for me when I started college? That kept track of my money and what I spent it on and stuff?"

Lexi shrugged. "Of course."

It had been her way of helping her brother, trying to apologize for not being able to go to college with him like she wanted to; like they'd talked about doing when they were younger. She'd learned plenty of accounting tips from her mother over the years and Excel was something she played with on the nights she couldn't sleep.

Not that her brother needed any help with math - he was a math teacher. But the spreadsheet did the math automatically and was a lot more convenient.

"There's this lady I teach with, she is the science teacher. Started a business this summer selling candles and I guess it got a lot bigger than she was expecting. Now that school has started again, she's having trouble keeping up with that and teaching. She's looking for someone to help her out, organizing the money for one thing."

Lexi tried to think rationally about this, when inside her all that she could feel was excitement. It was something she could actually do, maybe make a couple dollars in the process. "I can try it out," she said, trying to contain her interest. "It's not like I'm busy with other things."

Drew chuckled, feeling the excitement radiating off of her. Not that she could hide anything from him anyway, nor could he hide anything from her. It was a twin thing, as her mom had always said. And they had always been close; especially since Lexi's accident.

"I'll give her your contact information and then you can talk to her about it," Drew said as he looked out at the sky. "It's so warm out, how do you stand it?"

Lexi laughed as she looked down at her leggings and sweatshirt. "I'm always cold, so right now I'm actually comfortable," she replied as she pulled her legs up into her chair so she was sitting cross legged. "That is why I love summer. Unless it's like 90. Then I'll get an awful migraine."

Drew shook his head. "I hate to break it to you, but it isn't summer anymore. If it was still summer then I wouldn't be teaching every day."

"Let's be real, when aren't you teaching?" Lexi raised her eyebrows and they both laughed.

Growing up, Lexi hadn't always been able to make it to school. And on the days that she could make it to school; she hadn't always been able to pay attention well or stay the entire day.

Drew had been the one to go over all the lessons with her carefully. The one to make sure she understood everything. He'd been the one to make sure they had all the same electives in high school so he could help her with them as well.

In short, he had been the reason Lexi had finished high school. And he credited her with being the reason he became a teacher.

"So, sharing a house with Natala again. I suppose I shouldn't come over too much, there will be too many women here."

Lexi slapped her brother playfully. "Stop that, you grew up with all of us."

"And I complained all the time. It's very difficult having two older sisters. You two were always bossy and annoying," Drew teased.

"Who are you calling annoying?" Natala asked as she stepped onto the patio.

Drew and Lexi glanced at each other, laughter in their eyes. "You, of course. You were a bossy older sister."

"Oh sure, I was the bossy one," Natala walked over and sat down with the pair. "As I recall, it was Drew who was always telling me what to wear."

"You always wore stuff that looked weird," Drew looked at his older sister in mock-disgust. "I was still your brother, even if I am younger. I didn't want people thinking I had a bad sense of style."

"I had a great sense of style," Natala protested.

"Had? At least now you realize the truth," Drew stood up, resting his hand on Lexi's wheelchair.

"Andrew Luna," Natala exclaimed, standing up. "What are you trying to say?"

Drew began to back up and Natala started to chase him. Lexi laughed as she watched her siblings chase each other around the yard, Daisy joining in. It was as if they'd slipped back in time for this moment.

Chapter 3

Lexi groaned and itched her shoulder. Sleep was something she needed, but her mind didn't seem to agree. Her whole body felt itchy despite her using the last of her energy to put lotion on it a couple hours ago. Her heart seemed to be racing out of her chest, on top of her head pounding. It was all common when Lexi tossed and turned instead of actually falling asleep.

Daisy, despite normally sleeping in her kennel, was laying across her legs. She'd sensed that her owner needed her help calming down or normalizing her blood pressure. Lexi wasn't sure which. Maybe it was both.

Lexi really did want to get some sleep, but at this point all she would accomplish from trying was scratching her skin raw. She sighed and reached for her phone where it was charging on her nightstand. It wouldn't make her head hurt any less, but it likely wouldn't make it worse either.

She opened the chess app she'd downloaded way back when she got her first phone. Playing chess probably wouldn't help her sleep at all. But it would distract her from the itching and maybe that would be enough for the exhaustion to take over and she would fall asleep as she played.

Her excitement over the possibility of a job was probably part of the issue. Her brain couldn't stop thinking about it no matter how much she tried. The pounding in her head steamed from that. Lexi blinked, trying to bring herself out of her thoughts.

"Rookieforlife is on." Lexi noted with surprise. She requested to play a game with him, then closed her eyes for a moment as she waited for him to accept. Maybe she should get out of bed. Sitting at her desk may wake her enough for it to be easier to fall asleep later.

Lexi's phone buzzed and she smiled as she saw her request for a game had been accepted. She was white, so she made the first move then waited for Rookie to make his. She noted the chat had lit up, indicating that she had a message.

Late night? Rookie has asked.

Lexi smiled. *Later than I want it to be.* She quickly typed back, then returned to the game to make another move.

Rookieforlife, as his username called him, had been playing chess with Lexi since she started. The first match they'd been randomly put together by the computer. After that, he'd requested to play with her again and again.

"Darn it, not my bishop." Lexi groaned. She and Rookie were evenly matched, which was probably the reason they still played each other after these years.

You're slacking Queen. Rookie had typed.

Lexi would have shook her head if she was sitting up. Because she was still in bed, she settled for burying it in her pillow for a moment instead. Her username on the chess app was QueenLuna, and Rookie had called her Queen in chat.

It's late at night, my brain isn't functioning as well as it could be. Doesn't mean you're going to win. Lexi typed back quickly, then resumed the game. Now she was determined not to lose.

After a couple more moves and banter in the chat, Lexi realized this game probably wasn't one she could win. Her new goal was to stalemate him. That was better than outright losing.

No stalemate, that should be considered cheating. Rookie's chat showed up and Lexi's eyes narrowed.

You have no idea if I'm trying to stalemate you or not. The point of the game is to win, I'm trying to win.

You can't win, you know that, so now you're trying not to lose. I've played with you enough times before that I can predict all your moves. Rookie typed back quickly, apparently more interested in the chat than the actual game.

All my moves? Every single one?

Absolutely. Every single one.

Lexi blinked, then went back to the game. She didn't know how to reply to that honestly; so she'd focus on the game instead.

Even though Lexi had been playing Rookie for years, they'd never shared personal information. All Lexi knew about him was that he was a man, and he lived in the same time zone as she did.

"For all I know he could be our neighbor," Lexi whispered, then scrunched her face. That probably wasn't it, considering her house was bordered by elderly couples. From the words he used and the way he typed; Lexi was guessing that Rookie was close to her age.

"I definitely cannot win this now," Lexi sighed as her last rook was taken captive. All that was left was her king, and she'd never be able to win the game with just her king. With another over-dramatic sigh, Lexi suggested they call it a draw.

I'm winning this, it's all stacked against you. Why do you think I'd accept a draw?

Lexi shrugged one shoulder as she read that message. *I'm too tired to play much longer. And we both know I'll just lead your pieces around the board long enough that you agree to my draw. I'm good at evading capture.*

I wish you weren't so good at that. Rookie typed back, then the screen flashed a "game over" at her as he accepted the draw. Lexi frowned. *What did that mean?*

Rookie disappeared from her online friend list.

Disappointment filled her as she set her phone back on her nightstand and rolled onto her back to the annoyance of poor Daisy.

***

When Lexi woke up the next morning, she groaned. Her head hadn't stopped pounding. If anything, sleeping made it worse.

"Maybe because I was laying on it." Lexi offered to Daisy as an excuse. The dog thumped her tail, as if that would help Lexi somehow.

She reached to her nightstand for her pill container. After grabbing the migraine pill out, she sat up slowly. "Daisy, water bottle." She told the golden retriever.

The dog hopped off the bed and trotted out of the room. She reappeared a moment later with a water bottle in her mouth. She jumped back onto the bed and dropped the bottle into her owner's outstretched hand.

Lexi opened the water bottle. "Good girl Daisy." She praised the dog. She took the pill, then closed her eyes and grimaced. Her head really hurt, and she had the whole day in front of her. "That pill had better work."

She moved her body so she was sitting on her bed against the wall, then pulled her blankets over her shoulders.

Daisy lay across her lap, her eyes watching her owner closely. Lexi closed her eyes and tried to keep her body calm. She knew stress would only make the migraine worse.

At least it wasn't a chess day. Today was her catch-up day - the day she tried not to plan anything. That way she could catch up on things she may not have been able to do the rest of the week.

"I'll apparently catch up on migraines," she shrugged. "Isn't that perfect, Daisy? Catching up on throbbing pain in my head? It's a good thing you are a dog, you don't have to worry about them. I don't think dogs get headaches at least."

After a half hour of sitting and sipping her water, Lexi was relieved to find a bit of the pressure had gone away. She was careful in her movements as she got dressed and ready for the day. She did not want to risk a relapse.

"What should I have for breakfast?" She asked after she'd wheeled herself to the fridge.

Opening the door, she scanned the shelves. Leftover salad and hamburgers from last night, a couple cups of yogurt, some queso that had been used for nachos one night. Nothing looked especially good. Nothing was calling her name.

She looked at the top of the fridge where the cereal was kept. Her head hurt too much for her to try climbing up and grabbing that. She was too short to just stand up and grab a box. And when things were kept up high, Daisy was no help.

"Where is Mom?" Lexi asked the dog as she looked around the kitchen. Her mom was usually awake before she was. She shrugged that thought off as Daisy disappeared and wheeled over to the pantry where she grabbed a bagel. Cream cheese sounded good.

After putting the bagel in to toast, Lexi grabbed the cream cheese and the everything bagel seasoning so she was ready when the bagel was.

"Good morning," Connie greeted Lexi as she walked into the room, Daisy by her side. "Did you get some sleep?"

Lexi shrugged as she spread cream cheese on her toasted bagel. "I think I got a little bit of sleep. It wasn't good sleep though; I have a migraine now."

"I'm sorry honey. You should make sure you drink a lot of water today. You've had two longer days so I suppose it isn't crazy that your body is protesting now," Connie paused and looked at her daughter. "Is the vacuum going to bother your migraine? I wanted to get that room ready for Natala."

Lexi shrugged. "Go ahead, I don't think it's going to make anything too much worse. Close the door though, just in case, that keeps the noise a bit less."

"Can do," Her mother studied her. "You do look a little paler than you normally do."

Lexi bit her lip as she shook everything bagel seasoning over her bagel halves. "Thanks Mom," She replied before putting the seasoning away.

Connie pulled the vacuum out of the pantry and made her way down the hall.

Lexi sat back in her chair and wondered why her mother wanted to get the vacuuming done now. It had seemed like it would still be a couple weeks before Natala moved back. Her sister hadn't seemed especially keen on moving back into the family house.

Chances were her mother was doing a lot of work for nothing, but that wasn't Lexi's problem. Her mother liked to take care of her children. If Natala took some of her energy that was less of it directed at Lexi.

Lexi took a cautious sip of her water and looked over at Daisy, who had laid down on her dog bed with a chew toy. "What am I even going to do today? Maybe brush you, but that doesn't take very long. I have to do something, or else I'll go crazy."

"You could write a novel," David said as he walked by and ruffled his daughter's hair. "Or paint a masterpiece. Maybe even write a pop song, you learned how to play guitar."

Lexi frowned as she finished the bite of her bagel. "Dad, I played guitar for a year, and that's when I was eight. I would have no idea what I'm doing now and besides, we don't have a guitar."

"That's the problem with that statement? You have a migraine Lexi, don't do anything crazy like making loud noises," Connie said as she brought the vacuum back. "You could fold some laundry for me. That shouldn't hurt your head too much, and it needs to be done." She closed the pantry door and turned to look at her daughter. "I'll be in my office if you need anything."

"Thanks Mom," Lexi mumbled through her bagel. Her mom didn't actually have an office, but she had a desk set up in her room. That's where she was most days, doing various accounting tasks for her various clients.

She watched her father as he walked around the kitchen, seemingly looking for something. "What are you doing at home?" She asked him as she brushed the seasoning off her hands.

"I left my laptop somewhere; I need it for a meeting this afternoon," David replied absentmindedly as he looked under the table.

Lexi used a napkin to hide her smile. Her dad's meeting was most likely with the auto shop's owner. Those meetings happened once a month, and that was about the only times her dad used his laptop.

"I think Mom put it by your books," Lexi said as she put her plate in the sink. "That or she may have put it into your car last night, did you check there?"

David frowned. "It could have been in my car the whole time?" He pulled his keys out of his pocket and walked out to the garage, making Lexi giggle.

She went to her room and sat down in front of her own laptop, wondering if using it today would actually be a good idea. It could make her head worse, or it could not change how it felt. Was it worth the risk?

Lexi's phone buzzed and she pulled it out of her pocket to see who was calling. "Hello?" She answered.

"Hey Lexi. Is Mom around? I tried to call her cell but she wasn't answering," Natala covered the phone and said something that Lexi couldn't understand.

Lexi glanced out her bedroom door to see her parent's closed bedroom door across from it. "Mom is working, if you text her then she will call you when she gets a chance."

"Oh, I didn't think about that. Thanks, Lexi."

"No problem," Lexi grimaced as a loud beeping came from Natala's end of the phone. "Have a good day."

"You too!" Natala called back loudly, then hung up the phone.

Lexi wasn't sure what that noise had been, but she was glad it was over. Where was Natala anyway? Interviewing for a position around here? Or headed back to Illinois?

Lexi shook it off, it didn't matter where her sister was. She opened her laptop, deciding to risk making her head worse and turned it on. She pulled up her calendar, something she'd made years ago to keep her organized and help her prioritize.

"The block party is tomorrow?" Lexi glanced out the window, wondering how it had gotten that late in the year already. It seemed like summer had just started. Now the neighborhood was having their back to school/end of summer party?

"I wonder if Mom remembers that. Do you think she does, Daisy? We need to take stuff for that, it's a potluck."

The dog's tail thumped against the hard plastic sides of her kennel where she was laying. Lexi smiled and pulled open an internet window, then began to search for recipes. One of her favorite things to do when she had the energy was experiment with new recipes. More often than not, it didn't turn out well. But every so often she found an amazing recipe.

Like that potato salad last year. Lexi opened Word and pulled up that recipe, glancing through to make sure they had all the ingredients. Maybe that was a possibility to take tomorrow night. She pulled her phone out of her pocket and texted her mom to ask if she remembered the party.

Lexi left the recipe up, then turned back to her search. "Summer block party foods," She read the name of the article aloud, then scrolled down.

Salad, Lexi frowned. *That isn't creative - or very smart. That dressing sitting out in the sun would taste awful.*

What's next? She continued to scroll, carefully pulling her legs into her wheelchair so she was sitting on them. Her legs hit the desk now and she was looking down at the computer, but it was better for her blood flow. *Macaroni salad, a classic but also basic.* Although now that she was looking at the pictures, it sounded delicious. *I'm sure someone else will bring that.* She thought, remembering the containers full of it that were usually left over at the end of the party.

She noted a couple more recipes that were just creative - summer themed - decorated cookies. Lexi didn't have the patience to spend decorating cookies. When they'd tried that growing up, she had half of them eaten by the time her siblings had finished decorating their first one. Lexi had a lot more fun making food than she did decorating food.

Lexi scrolled and found various trail mix recipes that she wanted to make but didn't have the ingredients for, before she found the recipe for chocolate chip dip. *You dip cookies in it? It's like adding sugar to more sugar.* She clicked the image to pull up the recipe.

"More sugar is something I can get behind, Daisy." She read through the recipe, glad to find they had all the ingredients. "Not that you can eat it, but I'll make sure to take some of your favorite treats."

A knock came on Lexi's door and she turned to look at it. "Yes?"

Connie walked into the room, holding her phone. "I just got your text. I had forgotten about the party, that's really tomorrow?"

Lexi shrugged and pulled up the calendar again. "That's what it says. You can always check Facebook if you doubt it, I think you've gotten it as an event before."

Connie sighed and sat down on Lexi's bed. "No, I believe you. I can't believe I forgot about that; I was so busy getting ready for Natala yesterday."

"I found a dip recipe that sounds really good. Like a chocolate chip cheesecake, but you dip the crackers into the cheesecake. I could make that, and maybe the potato salad from last year. That went over really well."

"It was quite a hit," Connie looked at her watch, then stood up. "I have a meeting with a new client in ten minutes. If you want to make the dip, go ahead and do it. But be careful using the mixer, it is loud and I don't want your head to get worse. I'll cut up the potatoes for that salad while I cut some for dinner tonight. We can worry about actually making it tomorrow." She walked out of Lexi's room and back to her own, mumbling as she went.

"Okay." Lexi shrugged and went back over to the recipe. She clicked the link, and typed it into her phone. Then she used her phone to read the directions from and type them into a word document.

It was easier for her to have all her recipes look the same, and have no picture on them. Not to mention it took less ink and less space on the page when she typed it herself and omitted the unneeded information.

Lexi clicked print on the recipe, and saved it to her laptop before she turned off her phone screen and put her phone back into her pocket. *What time is it?*

She glanced at the corner of her laptop. *10:56,* she read. That meant about an hour to lunch, so she could make the dip now, eat lunch, then take a nap. *That works.* She sighed as she made her way to the kitchen and pulled the recipe out of the printer.

A nap wasn't exactly what she wanted to do this afternoon, but she already felt her body telling her it was going to happen. She may as well plan for it. "Daisy, you can go chew your bone. I've got to move around a lot and I don't want you to be in the way."

Daisy, seeming to understand perfectly, walked over to her bed and curled into a ball. Her eyes kept careful watch over her owner as Lexi gathered ingredients and brought them to the table.

Lexi brought over a bowl and the hand mixer. She would have liked to use the stand mixer. But that required her to have the energy to either stand up as she used it or the energy to pick it up and move it to the table. As she had energy for neither, the hand mixer would have to do.

Lexi plugged in her hand mixer and used it to mix the cream cheese, before adding the butter, brown sugar, and powdered sugar. She mixed that together till it all looked the same, then turned the mixer off. There was a ringing in her ears now that made her wince. The mixer wasn't exactly quiet. She had forgotten her noise cancelling headphones in her room.

She glanced over at Daisy, who was watching her carefully from her bed. She must not have a crazy blood pressure right now or Daisy would be nosing her.

Lexi sighed and added a splash of vanilla to her dip, then the mini chocolate chips. She winced as she turned the hand mixer back on to mix everything together quickly.

After she finished with it, Lexi was quick to remove the beaters and put them in the sink. She then put the mixer back into its cupboard. "Let's see if it tastes good," she told Daisy as she grabbed a graham cracker from the box. She dipped it into the dip then took a bite, a smile coming to her face as she ate. "It's light, fluffy, sweet, and the chocolate chips add a bit of texture." She sighed happily, not noticing Daisy giving her a jealous look.

Lexi closed the box of graham crackers and took it to the counter, along with the dip. She carefully found a lid for the dip and put it in the fridge, then glanced over to the dog. "I'm sorry Daisy, was I supposed to share with you?" She asked with a giggle.

"I guess it is lunchtime. Do you want some lunch?" Daisy wagged her tail and sat down in front of Lexi's chair.

"Well not there, you are in the way of me getting you any food. I have to open the fridge." Lexi watched the dog, who didn't budge. "Daisy, excuse me." She put her hand on the fridge handle.

Before she could open it, Daisy scooted out of the way. "Good girl," Lexi told the dog as she opened the produce drawer of the fridge.

She pulled out a bowl of lettuce, already washed and shredded and set that on her lap. She also pulled out the silicone bags of carrots, cheese, celery, and peas. She took these and the bottle of ranch dressing over to the table, instructing Daisy to close the fridge door for her.

"Good girl," she told the dog as she heard the fridge close. "Can you bring your bowl?"

A moment later, Daisy appeared beside her. She was carrying her plastic food dish in her mouth. Lexi took it from her and set it on the table, opening her bowl as well. She added carrots, celery, and peas to both bowls. After adding dressing to her bowl and some sunflower seeds that had been sitting on the table, she put the ingredients away in the fridge.

"Here you go girl," Lexi told Daisy as she set the dog's dish on the floor, then grabbed a fork and began to eat her salad.

"What are you having for lunch?" Connie asked as she walked into the kitchen and opened the fridge.

"A salad," Lexi replied. "It seemed easy." She took another bite of her salad as Daisy finished her food. Her mom was going to comment on how it wasn't balanced enough, how she needed more. Lexi narrowed her eyes as she waited.

"Did you add any protein to that?" Connie asked as he walked over to inspect the salad. "You are not going to be filled up by eating vegetables."

"Mom, I'm an adult. Let me eat my food and worry about my own body please." Lexi interjected as she pulled her bowl closer to her body.

"But you are still my child, and I want you to eat right. There is some chicken left over from this weekend, why don't you add some of that to your salad?" Connie offered as she pulled the container of chicken out of the fridge.

"Mom, I'm fine. I was planning to have one of the burgers that was left over from last night after I finished this." Lexi took a bite of her salad and tried to ignore her mother and just enjoy her food. Her mother was trying to help her, and one of the ways she tried to do that was making sure Lexi always ate a lot of protein.

Lexi knew it came from a good place, but often felt some resentment towards her mom. She was old enough to take care of herself. Old enough to worry about her own food and make her own mistakes. It was hard to do that when she still lived with her parents though. Not that Lexi could move out if she wanted to; but it was easier to resent her mom's somewhat hovering nature than her chronic illness.

"Well, that works I guess," Connie replied, putting the chicken away and pulling out the burgers instead. "Maybe I'll have a burger as well, that does sound good." She glanced at the clock. "I have a half hour to eat, then I have to get back to work."

"Thanks for telling me," Lexi mumbled. Daisy nosed her, warning her that she needed to calm down. "It's okay Daisy, I'm going to have a hamburger." She told the dog with a couple pats on her head.

Connie put her hamburger in the microwave and stood in the middle of the kitchen, watching her daughter and the dog. "Do you want me to heat it up for you? Then all you have to do is eat it." Connie didn't wait for an answer before she pulled out a plate and added a hamburger patty. She switched out the hamburger patties in the microwave and pulled a bun out of the bag, preparing the first burger.

"Here you go. You should probably have some fruit too. A good, balanced diet," Connie said as she set the plate in front of Lexi.

Lexi glanced at Daisy, choosing not to reply to her mom. Maybe Natala coming home would help something, her mom could worry about someone else for a bit. If Natala even chose to live here. She picked up the burger and took a bite. Some ketchup dripped down her chin, making her frown and reach for a napkin.

"You finished that dip then?" Connie asked as he sat down at the table across from Lexi.

"Yeah, it's done. I put it in the fridge with a lid on it. The graham crackers to dip in it are on the counter," Lexi replied before taking another bite of her burger. She had to admit, a burger and a salad made a pretty good meal for a hot day.

"Perfect. I'll have all the ingredients prepped tonight, so you can make that potato salad tonight or tomorrow morning. Be careful at chess, you don't want to miss the block party."

"I'll be careful, Mom." Lexi frowned. "Why is the block party on a Thursday night? Wouldn't it make more sense for it to be a Friday night? Then people wouldn't have to worry about getting home to sleep for school and work the next day."

Connie shrugged, "I'm not sure, it's just always been on a Thursday night. Tradition, I guess? Maybe it's on purpose so people have to leave early."

"Maybe," Lexi replied doubtfully.

***

"What should I do to stay awake for the next hour?" Lexi asked her dog as she closed the bedroom door after lunch.

Daisy wagged her tail and got into her kennel, laying down with a groan.

Lexi frowned. "Thanks for rubbing it in my face that you get to sleep right after you eat. Stupid acid reflux." She sighed, wishing she didn't have to stay upright for the next hour.

"Maybe I'll fall asleep sitting up," Lexi mused as she opened her laptop and pulled up her chess website.

She wished there was something more productive for her to do, but her head hurt and she had no clue what that would be. At least playing chess would make her use her brain. That had to be somewhat productive, didn't it?

Lexi thought back to last night and the project her brother had mentioned. She hoped that Birdie would contact her. Having a project would be a great change.

She wasn't sure if it would be a quick, one-time project or something she'd be able to do on a regular basis. Hopefully she could do it on a regular basis, and make a bit of her own money in the process.

"My head hurts, Daisy. I shouldn't have used that hand mixer; the sound really bothered me."

Daisy left her kennel and put her nose on her owner's leg, offering her a doggie look and kiss. Lexi gave the dog a small smile. "Thanks, Daisy. You're a great dog, you know that?"

Daisy's tail thumped on the outside of her kennel, bothering Lexi's head a little bit more. She sighed and backed up. She climbed into her bed and sat up against the wall. Using the computer wasn't a smart idea, though it would have kept her from boredom. Maybe falling asleep while she sat in bed was her best idea. A nap may make her head hurt a little less.

Daisy jumped onto the bed and lay across Lexi's legs, watching her owner closely. "I'm okay Daisy, I just need to breathe and try to stay calm." She reassured the dog.

The dog continued to watch her, making Lexi wonder if she ever got bored. Her job was to keep track of Lexi and help her if she needed anything. Surely that got boring after a while.

Lexi had gotten Daisy five years ago, when she was a puppy. She and Drew had done a lot of research on training service dogs before they got her, so they were prepared. Or as prepared as they could have been. Potty-training a puppy was no joke.

"You turned out perfectly didn't you Daisy?" She asked the golden retriever. They had taken her to plenty of obedience courses, and done plenty of training on their own as well. Lexi had to admit most of the training had been Drew's doing, and he'd done well.

"It's because you are so smart," Lexi told the dog as she petted her ears. She reached over to her nightstand for her water bottle and took a sip of that. After stacking some pillows on her side, she leaned against the wall and closed her eyes. She continued to pet Daisy, willing herself to fall asleep. Or for the migraine to suddenly disappear, she wasn't picky really. She just wanted to be able to function. It was something so simple for most people; but she wasn't most people.

Chapter 4

"All I really did yesterday was make a dip for my neighborhood's block party." Lexi admitted to Patsy after the chess club. "I took a nap. Then I couldn't get up. I was worried I wouldn't be able to make it tonight but last night's sleep gave me a little bit of my life back."

"I'm sorry hun. Didn't you just start on a new medication?" Patsy asked as she pulled the drawstrings of a bag of chess pieces closed.

"Not a new medication, an increase to the one I am already on. My neurologist was hoping it would help with all these migraines I'm having," Lexi explained as she rolled up one of the chess boards.

"Is it helping at all?" Pasty asked. She'd known Lexi through many different medications, doses, and symptoms. Over the years Patsy had been someone Lexi could rant to.

"It's only been a week, so it might be too soon to tell. So far, it hasn't changed anything, better or worse. But normally it takes a good two weeks for me to really get a feel for my medications," Lexi said with a sigh, stowing the chess board away. "I'll figure it out, I just wish I wouldn't wake up with the migraines."

"Do you know why you wake up with them? I know some of your triggers, like heavy perfumes you've had trouble with in the past, but what triggers one you wake up with?" Pasty asked as she put the lid on the first of the bins that was labeled "Chess Club".

Lexi shrugged as she backed away from the bin so Patsy could move it. "I might have done too much yesterday. Or the day before, because yesterday I didn't do anything. I'm not completely sure."

"I'm really sorry Lexi," Patsy told her as she stacked a second bin on the first. "I remember when you started the chess club, you were using a cane then. I was always impressed with how you carried yourself, as if your POTS was temporary and you were going to be better the next day."

She laughed as she saw Lexi cringe. "I know, I know. It is chronic, and there isn't a way for it to magically disappear."

Lexi gave her a small smile. "I don't even know what I'd do if I magically woke up one day cured. It's been my life since I was nine, I haven't had any practice with real world things. Like a job or college or whatever."

Patsy shrugged. "You'd figure it out."

"I guess so," Lexi agreed, glancing at the closed bins. They would be put back into the storage closet till the next chess club.

"Have fun at your party tonight!" Patsy told her as she picked up the bins.

"Thank you! Have a great evening," Lexi replied with a smile. "Daisy," She called. The dog trotted over from her spot in the corner.

You'd think that having a dog at chess club would be a big deal. That all the kids would want to pet her or something. Luckily, the chess club was full of some great kids. All of whom knew that she wasn't a pet. The service dog vest helped too, a very obvious reminded that Daisy was there in case Lexi needed her help.

"You're a big help, aren't you girl?" Lexi asked as she opened the car door for the dog and her wheelchair. "You keep a better eye on me than I do on myself." She got into the car and turned it on, checking in her mirror to make sure Daisy was settled.

"Do you want to come to the block party tonight? Or do you want some time at home?" Lexi asked the dog. She always took Daisy with her when she was going somewhere by herself. But if she was going with her mom or brother, especially to a busy or large place, she sometimes left Daisy at home.

Tonight, she would see how Daisy was doing. And see if Drew was planning to show up. He technically wasn't part of the block anymore and lived a couple blocks away. However, he had grown up there the same as Lexi and usually came back for the block parties. They were really just an excuse for the neighbors to get together, talk, and try each other's food.

The kids would play yard games, something Lexi had once eagerly participated in. The first year after her concussion, it had felt like a huge loss to not participate with the other kids. Natala had stayed with Lexi that night, insisting she was too old to play the kid games.

That was many years ago; now Lexi was used to being the odd one out. Anywhere she went she rarely noticed the attention her wheelchair or Daisy brought, because it was normal now. There were some days or moments that she noticed. There were some days and moments she felt sorrier for herself than others too, or she'd feel a bit depressed.

"Not that fun of a normal to have, Daisy," she told the dog as she pulled into the driveway. She sent a quick text to Drew to see if he was coming tonight before she got out of the car.

"I'm home, Mom," Lexi called as she walked in the front door, leaning her wheelchair against the wall. She sat down on the couch and glanced at the pile of mail that was on the side table.

"How was chess?" Connie asked from the kitchen. She was drying dishes from the looks of it.

"It was chess. Same stuff. Do you know if Drew is coming to the party?" Lexi asked as she flipped through the mail, checking to see if anything interesting had come.

Connie shrugged as she set a pot down on the counter. "I have no idea, but my guess is he will be there," she started drying a bowl. "He normally comes to these things. I should make sure to add a sign to the potato salad so everyone knows that's safe."

"Oh, the dip isn't," Lexi sighed. "I didn't even think about it being for the party when I dipped a cracker into it. Please don't mark that."

Drew was very allergic to gluten. So allergic a single crumb would make him sick. Lexi knew that, and had grown up being careful to keep crumbs out of things. However, that had faded quickly after he had moved out. When it wasn't a daily worry, it seemed to slip her mind.

"I would have remembered a lot easier if he was around. I probably would have thought of it tonight."

"It's okay honey, Drew understands. I have some of those cupcakes I'll take for the gluten free people of the neighborhood. They are in the freezer right now. I made them last month for something..." She set the bowl down and looked at the ceiling.

"For your birthday." Lexi reminded her with a laugh.

"Oh, that," Connie sighed and picked up another dish to dry. "I knew it was something like that."

"You just didn't want to admit you aged another year," Lexi teased her mom as she stood up and glanced at the clock. "I'm going to sit in the dark of my room for an hour. That will give me a break from stimulation for a while, maybe I'll make it through the whole party tonight. Please wake me up in time if I fall asleep."

"Sounds good," Connie replied as Daisy and Lexi walked down the hall.

After Lexi's self-proclaimed hour of quiet and darkness, she turned the lights on in her room and opened her closet. Could she go to the block party in her normal sweatshirt and leggings? Absolutely. Did she want to? Not particularly. It was one thing to feel like an absolute mess, Lexi tried not to look like one on top of that.

She pulled out a sundress and slipped that on, then grabbed a pair of boots. "What do you think Daisy? Do these boots cover up the fact that I'm wearing compression leggings?" Lexi asked the dog as she inspected herself in the mirror.

Her compression leggings were a nude color, but only went to her ankles. There was a clear difference there. The boots hid the fact that her feet looked a little paler color than her legs did. "They will work," she decided, pulling a pair of socks out to wear with the boots. Wearing socks would help keep her warm, which was helpful too.

Lexi grabbed a hairbrush and tried to neaten her hair. She pulled one side of it and twisted it up, then used bobby pins to keep it up on the side of her head. Standing there for a moment to make sure the bobby pins didn't hurt too much; she picked up her cane and a jacket. "Come on Daisy," she called as she left her room.

Lexi got into her wheelchair when she reached the living room, noting her dad was finishing drying the dishes. "You're home early," she commented. "I thought you'd just make it to the party."

David grinned. "There is free food, I'm not going to miss free food. I've had enough late shifts to make someone else work one for once."

"Not like I make any decent food here," Connie replied as she put her earring in. Lexi noted that she too, had changed into a sundress. She had done her makeup, something Lexi never bothered with.

"You look pretty Mom."

"Why thank you honey," Connie replied with a smile. She looked at Daisy, who was missing her vest. "Are you taking Daisy with you?"

Lexi shook her head. "Drew said he will be there. You and Dad will both be there. I'll keep my phone close and I'll be fine. Besides, the majority of these people will go running to you if they see me having any problem anyway. Daisy likes her breaks. She deserves them every once in a while."

Connie shrugged. "If that's what you want. Ready to go?" She asked David.

He stood up. "Sure," he replied, walking over to Lexi and picking her up

"Dad!" She shrieked with a giggle.

"It's a bit easier on your body than walking, dear daughter. And you are very light," he replied with a chuckle.

Connie - who was carrying the food - opened the door for them.

"Thanks Dad," Lexi said with a shake of her head. Maybe she should be embarrassed to be carried by her dad as a grown woman, but it made her feel like a little girl again.

She never brought her wheelchair to the block party, there was too much grass for it to be convenient. She had her cane, and if her dad carried her there that was more energy she could use to walk around if she chose.

"Anytime," David said as he tipped his hat to her. "Let's be off now."

Lexi rolled her eyes. Her dad must have had a good day at work, because he seemed to be in a very good mood. Or maybe it was the promise of free food that made him happy.

The party was held at one of the houses on their street. The house of an elderly couple and their daughter that had started it back when the daughter was a child. They had a small house, with one of the biggest backyards Lexi had ever seen.

That backyard was currently full of tables, chairs, and yard games that had come from various neighbors. Each was labeled with the family's last name in sharpie somewhere on the object. Occasionally she and her siblings had made a game of guessing which chairs belonged to which family.

"Thanks Dad," Lexi repeated once her father dropped her into a chair on the edge of the yard. It was a smaller table, set up for only four people. Lexi didn't mind being on the edge of things and just watching. It was interesting to see everyone who came. And to see how much they'd grown since she'd seen them last.

"Did you get the email from Birdie?" Drew asked a moment later as he sat down beside her and set a plate in front of her.

Lexi laughed; not surprised Drew had gotten there before they had. "Thank you for bringing me food," She replied, examining the plate. It all looked delicious, and seemed to contain mostly jello salads- her favorite food group. Drew knew her well.

She blinked when she realized what Drew has said. "I haven't checked my email for a couple days."

Drew sighed. "I keep telling you Lexi, you have to check it at least once a day. You'll miss out if you don't." He took a bite of potato salad.

"Birdie sent me an email?" Lexi asked, mentally sighing. *Why hadn't she thought to check her email? How long had the email been there and she just didn't know to check for it?*

"I said that already. Job, wanted your contact information, she said she emailed you," Drew shook his head. "And you don't have email hooked up to your phone so now you'll have to wait till you get home to see what the email said."

Lexi sighed. "If I am even able to. I don't know how much energy I'll have left in me at that point," she took a bite of the red jello salad, surprised to find it was cherry flavored. She'd been expecting strawberries, but cherry was good too.

"Your fault. Check your email," Drew elbowed her teasingly. "Good potato salad, by the way."

"Thanks. My fingernail may have fallen into it at some point, hopefully you don't have to eat that," Lexi shrugged. "It would add some keratin or whatever."

Drew gagged on his potato salad. "Lexi!" He scolded, shuddering. "Gross."

Lexi smirked, feeling a victory coming. "Sorry," she replied. "Didn't mean to bother you."

Drew stared at his plate, as if he wasn't sure anymore if he wanted to eat. "Why do you make life difficult?" He asked her with a groan as he stood up.

"I keep your life interesting," Lexi reminded him before he walked away. She was guessing that he would eat the rest of his food in silence, away from her teasing. She had to get back at him somehow.

As Lexi ate, she looked around at all the other tables. Most of the people she recognized. Or at least she knew what house they lived in. There were some new faces too, some older and some babies.

The kids were all gathered in a huddle by the yard games. She wasn't sure what they were doing and couldn't quite tell what it was from far away, but it seemed one of the kids was holding something. A phone probably. That seemed to be the thing these days, kids on their phone.

When Lexi was a kid, they played the yard games that were around them, not the games on their phones. *Darn it, that makes me sound really old. I have to stop thinking that.*

"Hello." Lexi was surprised to hear a deep voice from behind her.

"Hello," Lexi greeted, noticing a man. He had the greenest eyes that she'd ever seen. She'd never met him before. Maybe he was the son of someone from the neighborhood. *But where did those eyes come from? No one in this neighborhood.*

"Can I sit here or is this seat taken?" The man asked.

Lexi looked at him curiously. "It's available," she replied with a shy smile. He was so cute, why was that the first thing she noticed?

"I'm Cameron. Not actually from this neighborhood, but someone invited me to this gathering." The man explained as he set down his plate, then sat down in the chair beside Lexi. "Do you people-watch from here?"

Lexi laughed. "Yes, I people-watch from here. I do live in the neighborhood and I've been going to these things since I was a baby. I'm Lexi, by the way."

"Lexi," Cameron repeated.

Why did her name sound so good when he said it? Lexi mentally facepalmed herself for thinking that and tried to focus her attention on her food and the people she was watching.

"Is that short for something? Or is your full name just Lexi?" Cameron asked as he raised his burger to his mouth.

"Alexica. It's short for Alexica, which sounds way too..." She trailed off as she tried to think of the word. She was convinced her mom had only named her Alexica so it was a cute twin name that matched her brother's - Andrew. Joke was on her, as both children went by nicknames.

"Pompous?" Cameron suggested. "Proper, formal?"

Lexi laughed. "Maybe all of those. It gives me the jealous mean girl from a movie vibe. Like oh, watch out for Alexica. She'll try to steal your boyfriend."

"Steal many boyfriends in your day?" Cameron raised an eyebrow as he studied Lexi.

She felt her face heat up. "Not even close. I was never a popular kid. Maybe that's why I've always gone by Lexi. It's a little more girl who blends into the background vibe." Lexi ducked as a soccer ball came flying towards her table. Apparently, the kids had left the phone behind and picked up the real games now.

"Careful," Cameron watched as the ball landed on the ground a couple feet behind the table. "That could have ended a lot worse."

I've had things end worse than that. Lexi thought to herself, remembering falling out of the tree. "Maybe I'm not a background character if there are balls flying towards me."

"You could never be the background character," Cameron told her, watching her closely. "I think you'd be the main character."

Lexi laughed and tried to ignore how hot her cheeks felt as she picked up her fork. "I'll settle with just being a person living her life," she looked around the yard and noted her parents were at a table eating with their next-door neighbors and Drew.

So that's where he'd snuck away to. Served him right, Mr. and Mrs. Earnest were gossips, and they loved to talk. Drew would have been better off with her teasing.

"I forgot to get a drink," Cameron commented as he used a napkin to clean his hands. He glanced over to Lexi's empty plate. "I'm going to go grab something to drink, can I get you anything?"

"Lemonade would be wonderful, thank you," Lexi smiled again, wondering if her cheeks were enjoying this workout. She didn't normally smile that much. *There was something about this man...*

Cameron took Lexi's plate and his own and walked over to the drink table, giving Lexi a chance to watch him without being too obvious. He seemed tall, easily taller than Drew. Not that it took that much. Drew was what, Lexi frowned as she tried to remember, five foot four or something? Despite still being short, he was the tallest in their family. Both she and Natala were five foot two.

She blinked and looked back at Cameron. Did it matter how tall he was? When she was in her wheelchair anyone was taller than her. Even the elementary students that came to the chess club seemed to have some height on her. Cameron's hair was straight and a dark shade of brown, it seemed to be styled effortlessly in almost a curl on his head.

"Why am I thinking about this?" Lexi asked aloud, wondering where Daisy was when she needed her. Daisy was her best friend, the one she confided in. The dog was naturally a great judge of character.

"Here you go," Cameron handed her a red solo cup of lemonade.

"Thank you," Lexi accepted the glass and took a sip, glad for the drink. She should have brought her water bottle with her. That had completely slipped her mind tonight.

"Do you have any pets?" She asked Cameron. Before she admitted to anyone – even herself – that she liked this man she had to know if he liked dogs. Daisy wasn't negotiable.

"Not yet," Cameron grinned. "I just bought a house a month ago. Before that I always had an apartment. I wasn't allowed to have pets in the apartments but now that I can, I'm going to get a dog. Do you have any pets?"

"I have a golden retriever, Daisy. She's my best friend." Lexi replied, purposely omitting the fact that Daisy was also her service dog. Maybe she was enjoying the moment. Enjoying that a guy seemed interested in her for once. That may disappear as soon as he found out she wasn't quite what she seemed.

"What do you like about having a golden? I've been researching breeds and trying to figure out which would work best for me. They all have such different personalities."

That started a natural conversation about dogs and dog breeds, something Lexi was happy to talk about. Something that was normal for her to talk about, making her forget who she was talking to and just enjoy the moment.

Talking about dogs started the conversation and after that it just continued on various topics. Lexi was surprised when she realized the backyard had started to clear.

She looked down at her watch, noting two hours had passed. "It's getting late," she commented, then silently cringed at how that sounded.

"It is," Cameron noted as he checked the time on his phone. "I should make it back home and get some sleep before work." He typed something into his phone, then looked at Lexi as he slid it over to her. "Can I get your phone number? Maybe text you sometime?"

Lexi felt a blush sweep across her cheeks as she picked up his phone, feeling a bit weird about it. There was something almost intimate about typing in someone else's phone. She typed in her number quickly then handed him back his phone. "I'd like that," she replied shyly.

Cameron hopped off his chair, and Lexi noted her parents were packing up the dishes they had brought. "Thanks for talking to me. It was fun," she told Cameron with a smile. "I hope we can do it again."

With that, she slowly got up from her chair and grabbed the cane that had been leaning against the edge of the table. She walked over to her parents, not looking back.

Lexi didn't want to think about it, didn't want to see any thoughts of regret etched across his face when he learned she was broken. "Ready to go?" She asked her mom with a forced smile.

"I think so, I should have all the containers. Do you want dad to carry you?" Connie asked as she watched Lexi lean against her cane.

"No. I've been sitting all night, so I'm doing okay. I'll go to bed as soon as we get home. I can handle the loss of energy it takes me to walk a couple doors home."

"I get to escort two lovely ladies home? I really won the lottery today," David wiggled his eyebrows with a chuckle. He grabbed the last of the food they'd brought, then began to lead the way home. "Did you have a good time Lex? I noticed you didn't talk to many people."

Who needed to talk to multiple people when the one she'd spoken to had been so intriguing? Lexi thought. "It was fun Dad. Nice to be outside, I did a lot of people watching."

Chapter 5

When Lexi got home, Daisy greeted her eagerly with a wagging tail. She begged to be petter by brushing against Lexi.

"Were you a good girl?" Lexi asked the dog as she sat down on the floor. As she gave the dog a belly rub, Daisy's tail made a thumping sound as it tapped the floor.

Daisy lay down in her lap and gave her a doggie grin. David laughed. "It's almost as if your dog likes you or something Lexi," he said as he walked over to the kitchen and set down the empty dishes.

"Lexi, I want to get dishes done in the morning," Connie told her daughter as she looked at her phone. "I don't have a meeting until 10, and I'm too tired to do them tonight. I could use your help drying."

Lexi shrugged as she continued to pet Daisy "Okay," she agreed. Hopefully she'd be able to get up and eat some breakfast first. She missed when Drew had lived at home. Then she'd only had to help with the dishes every other day.

Speaking of Drew... Her eyes widened as she remembered the email Drew had mentioned.

"Daisy, up," she told the dog, then used her as a support to stand up herself.

"I'm going to bed," she told her parents before making her way to her bedroom, Daisy in tow. Once she was inside, she closed her door and made a dash to her laptop, a speed she rarely moved at.

"Come on, come on. Internet you have to work right now!" Lexi couldn't hide her eagerness. If Birdie had emailed her that had to be a good sign, right? Someone wasn't going to email just to say they weren't interested in working with her.

The email popped up along with a couple junk ones, the library's weekly newsletter, and a random study her mom had forwarded her. Lexi bypassed all the other emails and opened the one that was from Birdie12.

She scanned it, reading so fast she had to read a second time before she understood. Birdie asked if they could meet sometime to talk about what exactly needed to be done. And Birdie could get to know her that well. She asked if Lexi would be free Friday night or Saturday at all and noted that she wasn't allergic to dogs and hoped Lexi would bring the service dog Drew talked about.

Lexi felt a smile come to her face. "She wants to meet us, Daisy, both of us. And maybe I'll be able to help her out." She pulled up the google maps website and typed it in the address. It seemed Birdie lived about ten minutes away from Lexi.

Lexi went back to her email and typed out a reply, trying to sound professional and convey her interest at the same time. She added that she was available both tomorrow night and Saturday. Lexi read through the mail and grimaced, then added "Is your house wheelchair accessible?" Before signing and sending the email.

She hated to ask people if their homes were wheelchair accessible. She didn't like to ask anyone to do more work to accommodate her. But especially tomorrow night she would likely be tired enough she'd need her wheelchair. Lexi took a deep breath in, then breathed out. She reached down to pet Daisy, who had been nosing her. "I'm okay girl, I think my adrenaline is just completely out of whack now."

Lexi grabbed her phone and backed her desk chair away from her desk. Her heart felt like it was racing through her chest. She could feel the adrenaline coursing through her veins. Someone else would probably feel this way after completing a marathon, but for Lexi it could happen by just standing up. Excitement and anticipation would normally send her into a pretty long adrenaline spiral, and she was guessing that was what this one would turn into.

Lexi's phone buzzed, making her jump in surprise. Her phone dropped out of her hand onto the floor. Putting her hand on her heart overdramatically, Lexi took a couple breaths. She was really hyped up now; not that she needed to be. It would have been a good time to sleep.

"Phone Daisy," Lexi said, pointing to the phone. Daisy used her mouth to pick up the device and hand it to her owner.

Lexi tried not to grimace at the dog slobber on it. She used her dress to wipe it off, glad at least that she hadn't had to bend down and get it herself. That may have made her faint tonight.

Lexi pushed the home button. She was surprised to find a text from an unknown number. She typed in her passcode and opened the message.

Hey Lexi, this is Cameron. I really enjoyed talking to you tonight, I'd love to do it again sometime. Maybe go out for coffee if you're interested?

Lexi blinked. Then she read the message again. Was this real? How could she be sure it wasn't her brother pranking her? Her mind went back to the few dances in high school, she'd been asked to almost all of them by some boy as a "joke".

She scrunched her nose as she remembered Drew hadn't met Cameron, he wouldn't know his name to be able to prank her like this. Nor would he, she admitted. He knew this kind of prank would be more hurtful than funny.

Hey Cameron, I really enjoyed talking to you as well. She typed, then stared at the screen. She wasn't sure what to say next. Did she offer up a time? A place? Was she crazy for wanting to go out with this man? He'd just leave her when he realized she wasn't normal. She took another breath before typing *I'd like to get coffee* and sending the message.

She didn't have to wait long for a reply; it seemed Cameron had been watching for her message.

Great! I was a bit afraid I'd scare you off by texting too soon. I've been told you are supposed to keep people guessing and make them wait, but I feel a bit too old for that. I'd rather be direct. Are you available this weekend at all?

Lexi read the message aloud to Daisy. "What should I say girl? Do you want to meet him?" She paused. "You are going to meet lots of people this weekend. And new places."

Daisy gave a wag of her tail in response, seemingly unfazed by the thought of meeting more people. It wasn't Lexi's favorite thing to do. Her dog was a lot more outgoing than she was.

I like your directness. I may already have something planned Saturday, I haven't heard back yet. Will Sunday work?

Sunday would work great, but I'd love to see you sooner. Can we wait until you hear back on your plans to set a date for the date?

Lexi felt herself blush. The adrenaline rush was definitely in full swing, she wasn't going to get any sleep tonight. *Sure, I'll let you know as soon as my plans are figured out.*

Perfect. I look forward to hearing from you.

Lexi smiled at that text, then opened her chess app. Maybe chess would calm her down. That made sense somehow, right? She was happily surprised to see Rookieforlife was on, and clicked the button to ask him if he wanted to start a game.

Daisy nudged her leg, and Lexi looked down at the dog. Daisy eyed her, as if trying to talk through them.

"What is wrong?" Lexi asked the dog. She knew Daisy was trying to alert her to something. She just wasn't sure what that something was.

Daisy nudged her again, her wet nose tickling Lexi. She frowned and scooted her chair over to her bedside table. She picked up her blood pressure cuff and put it on, pushing the button to check her blood pressure.

A moment later it beeped at her. She wasn't surprised to see the screen was red, indicating she was in dangerous territory. It was lower than it should be. Lexi sighed and grabbed a packet of electrolytes to add to the water bottle sitting on the table. "I'll drink them Daisy, I promise. You did a good job girl."

Lexi mixed the packet into her water and took a big sip, and another. She carefully drank the entire bottle of water, then set it down on her bedside table.

"Here is a treat for you Daisy, you did a great job," she praised the dog again. Daisy wagged her tail and took the treat. She sat down at Lexi's feet to eat it, telling Lexi her blood pressure hadn't been magically fixed. If it was normal again Daisy would have gone into her kennel.

She shrugged it off. She'd done what she could. Time was what she needed now. Maybe the adrenaline rush would disappear as well. She picked up her phone again, noting that there was a game in progress, and Rookie had already made his move.

She moved a pawn, then opened the blinking chat button.

Queen? Are you there? Rookie had typed.

Sorry, I needed water. I'm here now, I think I can win tonight. Lexi typed back. She clicked back to the board. Rookie had made a predictable move; she knew exactly how to counter. It was an opening he used a lot; one they'd practiced today in the chess club.

I don't think water is going to give you an advantage. Rookie typed back, making Lexi laugh.

The water had nothing to do with it, I can beat you without that. She leaned back in her chair, settling in for a long game. He seemed ready to play, and she was plenty alert. It seemed like there wouldn't be too many stupid mistakes by either of them tonight. It would be an evenly matched, competitive game of chess.

***

Lexi woke up the next morning feeling not terrible. She never felt great when she woke up, but this was better than most mornings. She stretched, happy to see Daisy was still asleep in her kennel.

Lexi sat up slowly, then scooted over to her desk. She pulled up her email and signed in. The three seconds it took to load seemed like forever as she tapper her fingers on the desk impatiently.

"She replied Daisy!" Lexi exclaimed as she saw an email from Birdie. She immediately opened it.

Glad to hear you are interested! 7pm tonight would be great if that works for you.

I look forward to meeting you!

-Birdie

Lexi shrugged, then quickly replied that 7pm worked great for her. She added that to her calendar, then sat back in her chair. Daisy yawned from her kennel. Lexi smiled as she watched the dog stretch, then blink.

"Good morning," Lexi greeted. "We are going to go meet Birdie tonight."

Daisy blinked at her a couple more times before slowly exiting her kennel. She stood and waited as she watched Lexi. She was probably trying to figure out if Lexi would be feeding her this morning or if she should go find Connie.

"I need to get dressed first," Lexi told the dog as she stretched her arms above her head. "Give me a moment or two, then we can go eat."

Daisy wagged her tail as if she understood, and lay down by the door. She waited for Lexi to get dressed and brush her hair before she stood up again.

Lexi led the way out of her room, Daisy not leaving her side. She made her way to the living room and sat down in her wheelchair. "Okay Daisy, let's get you fed. Then I'll figure out what I want to eat."

"I'm making hard-boiled eggs. You can put some toast in to go with them if you want," Connie told her from the kitchen.

Lexi glanced at Daisy. She wished the knowing glances worked as well with canines as they did with siblings. "Okay," she replied as she fed Daisy. She added a piece of toast to the toaster. "Do you want toast too?" She asked before putting it down.

"Sure, that would be nice," Connie replied as she stirred the eggs on the stove.

Lexi added another piece of toast to the toaster, then sat back down in her wheelchair with a sigh.

"I have a meeting tonight at 7," she announced as she opened the fridge and pulled out the butter. "Someone Drew knows and recommended I help out with some accounting or something. I'm not completely sure but it would be nice to eat and have dishes done before that."

"That's wonderful that you are getting out honey. Maybe you'll make a new friend, you could use a couple of those," Connie replied. "We can eat dinner at 5. That way dishes and everything will be done well before 7."

Lexi rolled her eyes. Of course, her mom missed the part completely about it possibly being a job. In her mom's mind she was still a teenager, probably always would be.

It was a struggle for Lexi, because in some ways she felt like she was still a teenager. She loved her mom and appreciated all that both her parents did for her, but some days she just wished for her own space. *Of course, affording my own apartment is just a dream*, she acknowledged in her thoughts.

Lexi pulled out her phone, intending to text Drew. He'd be excited for her at least. He knew how much this opportunity meant to her. She typed out a message and clicked send. Before she could put her phone back into her pocket, it buzzed.

Lexi blinked. That couldn't have been Drew, he should be busy teaching by now.

"The toast is done," Connie told her as she turned off a burner.

Lexi put her phone away and pulled the toast out of the toaster. She put each piece on a plate, then buttered them. "Are the eggs ready?" She asked as she carried the plates to the table.

"One moment," Connie replied, cracking one of the shells.

Lexi filled her water bottle and set that on the table. She smiled at Daisy. "You finished all your food already girl? You must have slept well." She opened the sliding door and the dog ran out to the backyard.

"Here are your eggs," Connie said as she set a bowl in front of Lexi along with a fork. "I made a list on the fridge of things that could use doing today. If you get a chance, that is. I don't want to tax you too much."

"I can try. I'll help with the dishes after breakfast," Lexi said as she picked up her fork and began to eat.

***

Lexi spent her day carefully, trying not to use up too much of her energy. She cleaned out the fridge and knocked one of the things off her mom's list. She made herself and Daisy lunch. Then found herself taking a nap. It wasn't a conscious choice. When her eyes started closing as she played chess on her laptop, she let herself fall asleep.

Lexi finished dinner and dishes, then loaded up herself and Daisy into the car. "Ready to go Daisy? This could be a big thing," she told the dog as she typed the address into the car's GPS system. She clicked begin, then buckled up her seat belt and pulled out of the driveway.

Her drive was mostly silent, except the quiet panting Daisy did. She was lost in her own thoughts and worries.

When Lexi got to the address, she pulled into the driveway. She noted that there was a small ramp up to the front door. That was something she hadn't expected to see.

Lexi rang the doorbell. She wasn't sure what she was expecting, but the short redhead who answered the door wasn't quite it.

"Are you Lexi?" She asked with a smile, then shrugged. "Who else would you be? Come on in, I hope the smells don't bother you too much. I just finished a batch of the cinnamon sugar candles; I should have had them done yesterday." The woman closed the door behind Lexi and Daisy.

Lexi could smell cinnamon, and something sweet. Sugar, she supposed. It wasn't super strong, so hopefully it wouldn't bother her head. "You are Birdie, I'm assuming?"

The woman sighed. "I'm so sorry, I didn't even introduce myself. Yes, I'm Birdie. Actually, it's Beatrice, but the kids at school always called me Birdie and it stuck." She walked into another room; one Lexi thought was a kitchen under all the candles.

The table was covered in jars. A wick and something silver was coming out of each one. There was a short counter that held cardboard boxes and labels, along with a stack of paper that seemed about to fall over.

"ADHD, that's what they call it now. When I was a kid, I was simply labeled a troublemaker. I couldn't concentrate and I'd flutter from one thing to another - thus Birdie," The woman picked up a jar and studied it, then set it down. "I'll just grab a chair and sit, that's easier than trying to move these candles right now."

As Birdie walked down the hall, Lexi watched her. The woman seemed older than Lexi would have originally thought. She definitely seemed to have a young soul. Maybe that's why she was a teacher, the kids probably liked her. Lexi wondered if the red hair was natural. It seemed so close to orange Birdie could have passed for Ms. Frizzle.

"Okay," Birdie set down a chair across from Lexi and sat down, glancing at Daisy. "She's really well trained, isn't she? I'm impressed."

Lexi smiled. "She's an excellent help."

"Help is exactly what I need," Birdie frowned. "Well, not from the dog. You, I'm hoping." She handed Lexi a box that was full of what looked like receipts. "This is only my expenses. My accountant told me to save everything and total it for a tax deduction, but I have no time for that. Between teaching and actually making these candles..." Birdie trailed off as she looked at the table.

"That's a start. There are other things too that I could use some help with that would be similar. Totaling my sales, trying to calculate profit on sales, that sort of thing. All that you could do from your house, on your own time. I'd have you keep track of the hours you did work and I can pay you based on that. You can do whatever you can handle for hours." She smiled at Daisy.

"Drew told me about your health concerns. I don't think they would pose any problems. I won't really have deadlines so even if you have days that you can't work, it's fine. Anything you are able to do is less that I have to do." Birdie took a deep breath as she looked around her kitchen, then back at Lexi. "That is, if you're interested. I don't at all mean to take advantage of you, and you are free to say no. But when Drew mentioned it, I thought it might be a win for both of us." Birdie leaned forward in her chair, as if studying Lexi.

Lexi wasn't sure what to say. This was nothing like an interview. This was a job offer really. Birdie had said she would pay her.

Totaling receipts seemed simple enough to do in Excel, she could just make a spreadsheet and add all of them. The spreadsheet would even calculate the total for her. "I can try," she offered. "I've never done it for a business before, but I think I can. And the flexible hours would work perfectly for me, I have some days that I do more than others. And some nights I can't sleep."

Birdie broke into a big smile and gave Lexi a hug, much to Lexi's surprise. "I'm so glad Drew thought of this. I don't know what I was thinking, going into business and keeping a teaching career."

Lexi looked at the candles on the table. They weren't labeled yet. She couldn't read anything that was on the counter. "What is your business called?" She asked curiously. She should have asked Drew, so she could have looked it up ahead of time.

"Oh, bless me I should have started with that," Birdie laughed. "It's called Siena's Scents. I do all the making of the candles, but my business partner does the scent combinations. She has a nose for that."

Lexi tried not to visibly react. Drew hadn't mentioned anything about a business partner, wouldn't that change something? She'd be working for multiple people? That sounded more complicated. Was this something she should have put a little more thought into?

"Siena? Can you come here for a moment; I have someone I'd like you to meet." Birdie called down the hall. Lexi watched as a door opened and a girl came out.

She looked like she couldn't be more than ten, she was little. She had the same red hair that Birdie had, so Lexi was guessing it was natural.

Even more surprising? The wheelchair the girl was sitting in.

Chapter 6

"Siena, this is Lexi and her dog Daisy. Lexi is going to do some of my paperwork, you know, all the things I don't have time for." Birdie introduced. "Lexi, this is my daughter, Siena. She just turned thirteen and she is the scent master behind all these candles."

Lexi smiled at the girl. "It's nice to meet you," she told her. Silently, she wondered how she could be thirteen. She looked so fragile and little.

"Nice to meet you too," Siena said shyly, eyeing Daisy. "What does she do for you? Like can she open doors and stuff?"

Lexi laughed. Questions about Daisy were easy. "She can open doors, yes. She can also bring me things like my water and pills when I need them. She even gets my mom for me. That's a newer one. I don't have to directly give her a command. If I call for Mom or ask where Mom is, Daisy takes that as her cue to bring her to me." She patted the dog, who sat beside her wheelchair. "And she senses my blood pressure, so when it gets too high or too low, I can fix it."

"That's awesome," Siena breathed. "I keep asking Mom for a service dog, but she says they are expensive." The teen wrinkled her nose. "It would be so nice for her to carry my backpack around school. And she could turn on my lights and open my doors, some of that stuff is too tall."

Birdie sighed. "We moved into the house already built, because that was easier than building from scratch. So far, we have redone the kitchen so Siena fits perfectly. But some of the light switches are still too high for her to reach."

Lexi nodded as if she understood, but inside she could feel her heart breaking a little bit. She could stand up and turn on or off light switches if she needed to, but it seemed this little girl couldn't.

Siena shrugged. "Someday I'll get one," she announced. "After the candles are going well. I'll go to college and learn how to run a business, then I'll really help Mom. We can make a factory that is all wheelchair accessible and everything."

"That's the dream sweetheart, after you finish school." Birdie laughed before turning to Lexi. "I'll walk you out."

Lexi followed Birdie out the front door, the box of receipts still on her lap.

"I'm sorry, Siena gets very excited sometimes. I think she dreams of making the world a fully wheelchair accessible place." Birdie put a strand of hair behind her ear that had escaped its bun. "She's been in a wheelchair since she was five. She was born without the use of her legs. Paralyzed from the waist down."

"I'm sorry," Lexi whispered, now very unsure what to say. This wasn't how she'd expected the interview to go at all. Did Drew know about Birdie's daughter? Was that part of the reason he had recommended her for this job?

"Oh, don't worry about it. She has the biggest spirit I have ever seen and if anyone can change the world, it's going to be my little girl." Birdie smiled fondly then looked at Lexi. "So, are you interested? I can only pay a bit more than minimum wage to start."

Lexi had to bite her lip to keep from screaming in excitement. Minimum wage, or a bit higher, may not seem like much to someone else. To Lexi it felt like a fortune. It was a job, a real job that she could physically do. Something she could make her own money on.

"I'd love to," she answered honestly.

"Wonderful," Birdie sighed with relief. "Just keep track of your hours then, and I'll know how to pay you. I guess let me know your progress once a week? Maybe that's a good way to do it."

It seemed like Birdie was deciding as she spoke. Lexi was a bit shocked by how little thought the woman had put into this. Then again, that could just be because Lexi was the type to plan everything ahead of time.

"Yes, let's do that. You e-mail me a progress report every Friday, and we can see where to go from there." Birdie gave her final instructions.

"Sounds good," Lexi agreed quietly. "Thank you."

"Oh gosh girl, don't be thanking me. This is a huge help for me, I should be thanking you." Birdie smiled and walked back up the ramp. "Thank you for coming to meet me, I look forward to hearing from you next week."

Lexi watched as she went back inside, then looked down at the box in her lap. She went over to her car and hoisted the box up, along with her chair after Daisy had gotten in.

That had to be the weirdest interview in history, right? Lexi thought as she started her car. Either that or all the ones she'd read about in books had been weird. This one had no questions about her qualifications, no questions about previous jobs, no questions at all really.

Lexi was brought out of her thoughts by the vibrating of her phone, alerting her to a text message. *Probably Drew, wanting to know how it went.* Lexi thought as she began her drive home.

When Lexi got back to the house and made it inside, she was surprised to find the lights were off. She set her keys on the table and picked up the note that was there.

Lexi -

Dad and I went to catch a movie that is only playing in theaters today. I would have told you earlier but your dad surprised me with tickets when he got home from work. We will be home around 10 or 11, feel free to lock all the doors and just go to sleep. See you tomorrow!

-Mom

"They went to the movies," she explained to Daisy, who was looking at her as if also confused by the dark house. "So, I guess that means we go hang out in our room. I can't imagine sleeping right now." Lexi looked down at the box in her lap, realizing she could start these too.

She shrugged, then made her way to her room to get into some comfy clothes.

She pulled her phone out of her leggings pocket and threw it onto the bed before changing into fleece pajama pants. She frowned as she remembered the text she'd gotten earlier. It could have been her mom, telling her where they went. Or Drew, as she originally guessed.

Lexi finished putting on her pajamas. She grabbed her water bottle and phone and sat down at her desk. She unlocked the phone, surprised to find the text wasn't from Drew or her mother. It was from Cameron. A zing of excitement ran through her body as she read the message.

Good evening, I hope I'm not being a bother. I was wondering if you'd finalized your plans, if you are free tomorrow.

Lexi realized she'd forgotten to get back to him. *Who forgot to reply to a cute guy?* She sighed and looked up at the ceiling as if that would help.

She quickly typed her apology for not getting back to him sooner, before confirming that she was free tomorrow. She sent that, then waited a moment to see if the text would come as quickly as it had yesterday.

Apparently not, Lexi thought as she set down her phone and turned on her laptop. She backed up her chair a bit, then sat and tried to let her body relax. It didn't seem like she had too much of a headache. Her leg was tingling, but she didn't need that to play with Excel.

"I think I'm okay to work on the computer," she told Daisy, who had jumped up onto Lexi's bed to take a nap. The dog didn't respond, so Lexi took that as agreement.

She opened Excel and clicked on a blank workbook, then titled it Siena's Scents. Then she selected a sheet and labeled that expense receipts. Lexi shrugged, and pulled out a receipt. She looked at it and found the total. There was probably more to this than just writing totals. Did she need the dates? How much of this needed to be recorded? Did she need to categorize things?

With a sigh, Lexi turned to the place she usually got information from - the internet. She put the receipt back into the box and typed "How to log expense receipts for a business" in the search bar before sitting back and getting ready to research.

***

When Lexi heard the front door open, she was surprised to find three hours had passed. She had gotten so busy with this project she hadn't even thought about going to bed. Lexi looked at the receipt she held and added the total to the sheet. Then she set it in the finished pile. She saved the spreadsheet. She'd managed to enter three receipts, but now she should probably stop.

Lexi's headache was starting to catch up with her. She didn't want to cause any more problems for herself. She saved everything, then shut down her laptop.

Her parents probably assumed she was asleep by now. They didn't even stop outside her door. Lexi walked over to the light switch and turned off the lights, realizing she hadn't turned the Christmas ones on first. Oh well, she could find her bed in the dark.

"Daisy, bedtime," she told the dog.

Daisy dutifully jumped off the bed and curled up inside her kennel.

Lexi got into bed, laying her phone on the nightstand without looking at it. "Night girl," she murmured sleepily to her dog as she settled under the warm covers.

***

When Lexi awoke, she was surprised to find it was morning. Sleeping through the night was rare for her. She'd forgotten it was even possible. "Morning girl," she murmured sleepily to Daisy.

She grabbed her phone from the nightstand, still lying in bed. It was Saturday after all. What were Saturdays for if not to lay in bed for a while?

She noted there was a text from Cameron.

Are you interested in meeting for dinner at 6? Where do you enjoy eating?

Lexi smiled, holding her phone to her chest. She still wasn't sure she trusted Cameron. Maybe he'd just missed the cane she'd held. Maybe he assumed she sprained her ankle or something temporary. Either way, she had very much enjoyed talking to him and couldn't wait to do that again. Lexi pulled up her weather app and looked at today's predicted temperatures before she replied.

6pm would work just fine. I enjoy eating pretty much anywhere, but somewhere with outdoor seating would be great.

With Daisy, it was a lot easier to sit outside. Granted, Daisy was supposed to be allowed into any restaurant because she was a service dog. Some people still gave her weird looks or glared at her for daring to bring a dog. As long as it wasn't 90 degrees out, it was easier to just eat outside.

Lexi looked at the dog, who was sitting in her kennel watching Lexi. "Do you want to go out to eat tonight?" She asked the golden retriever.

Daisy's tail thumped against the side of the kennel, making Lexi smile. She buried herself a little more into her blankets, enjoying the comfort. "Come here girl," she whispered, patting the bed.

Daisy stood up, walked over to the bed and jumped up. She curled up beside Lexi like that was where she was meant to be. A moment later Lexi heard soft snores coming from the dog. She giggled. "Oh Daisy."

Her phone buzzed, and she unlocked it to view the message.

Franks? I've heard some great things about that place, I'm pretty sure it has outdoor seating.

Lexi smiled. Frank's Bar and Grill had great pizza and great burgers, both foods she enjoyed. And they always brought Daisy a bowl of water.

Franks would be perfect; I'll meet you there at 6. She replied. She contemplated getting out of bed, but the coziness of her bed and her dogs snuggles won out and before long Lexi had drifted back to sleep.

***

Lexi did not spend her entire day in bed. She only managed to sleep another half hour. Then she got dressed and ready for the day. She paid a little more attention to what she was wearing today, making sure her leggings weren't wrinkled and her shirt was clean. Sometimes she just grabbed a shirt she'd worn a day or two already. That was a lot easier than making more laundry to deal with on laundry day.

Lexi and Daisy ate breakfast, then spent some time making the pile of receipts smaller. Lexi was getting the hang of entering them. It was going a little faster now. By the time she needed to get ready to leave, she'd managed to get quite a few of them of them into the spreadsheet. She pulled up another spreadsheet she had designed for her hours, entered them in, then powered down her laptop.

"We need to get ready to go Daisy," she told the dog. Daisy cocked her head like she was listening. "I should run a brush through my hair at least," Lexi looked in the mirror, then picked up her brush. After spraying some dry shampoo through it, she brushed carefully. Then she grabbed a small section of hair on one side of her head and braided it quickly, then pinned it back.

"What do you think, girl?" She asked Daisy, turning around to get the dog's approval.

Daisy gave her a doggy grin, which Lexi took as a good sign. She grabbed her cane and water bottle, then left her room.

"Where are you going again?" Connie asked as she tried to leave the house.

"Frank's, Mom. I'm going to eat dinner, talk to a friend, then I'll be home. Daisy is with me, and you were the one to tell me I needed more friends. Bye." Lexi opened the backdoor and hurried out, not giving her mom a chance to protest.

She understood her mom's concern, but where had that been when she was going to a stranger's house yesterday? At least tonight it was a public, pretty popular restaurant. Maybe it was because Lexi was leaving the house two nights in a row. Other than going somewhere with her parents, chess club was one of the only things she left the house for.

Lexi hopped into her car after she got Daisy situated. She tossed her cane across the passenger seat. She figured she'd be sitting in a chair eating most of the night, so she could get away with just her cane. With restaurant doors, it was a lot easier not to have her wheelchair anyway.

Lexi tried to stop the nerves that came as she drove. That seemed impossible to do. For some reason, this guy had touched a string of her heart or something crazy. She was interested; she couldn't deny that.

"Here we are Daisy," Lexi whispered as she pulled into a parking spot and turned off the car. She spotted Cameron sitting at one of the outdoor tables, glancing around the parking lot. "I'm ready if you are."

Lexi took a deep breath in, then breathed out. Nerves were fine. That was probably expected for this situation. She could ignore them. She took one more deep breath, then grabbed her cane and opened the driver door.

As she opened the back door for Daisy, she didn't look at Cameron. She was curious what he was thinking, but at the same time she didn't want to know. Daisy's service dog vest made it pretty obvious what her job was.

"Hello," she said shyly as she walked over to the table Cameron had claimed. She noted there were already two glasses of water there.

He looked her up and down, then grinned. "Hello," he echoed. "Thank you for coming out with me. I already ordered a pizza. I hope that's okay."

Lexi smiled as she slid into the chair across from him, resting her cane on the table. "That sounds perfect," she replied, then gave Daisy the command to lay down. The dog did exactly as she was asked, eyeing Cameron carefully. It was as if she was trying to assess what risk he was to Lexi.

Secretly, Lexi was watching the dog to see if Daisy approved. It was a stupid thing to matter to Lexi, but she cared what her dog thought. Dogs seemed to have a judge of character that was much better than a human.

"This is Daisy," Lexi introduced, figuring she couldn't ignore the elephant in the room. Rather, the dog beside her. It would have to be addressed at some point tonight.

"She's beautiful," Cameron replied as he glanced at the dog.

Lexi smiled. "Thank you. She's my best friend." She saw the waitress coming with a pizza.

"Here you go, half cheese and half ham." The waitress smiled at Daisy as she set the pizza and plates on the table. "And I'll be back in a moment with a bowl of water for your dog."

"Thank you," Lexi said again, this time to the waitress. She eyed Cameron. "Half cheese, half ham? That's not an average pizza order."

Cameron grabbed a slice and put it on his plate. "I wasn't sure what your favorite was, but I figured cheese is something anyone would like. And ham is my personal favorite, so I couldn't resist that."

Lexi's nose twitched. "My favorite is ham as well," she said as she took a slice of pizza. She took a bite. She marveled at the taste of it, somehow Frank's always got the cheese right. It was warm and pulled like cheese should, but it wasn't hot enough to burn the roof of your mouth.

"Something else we have in common," Cameron commented, eating his own slice of pizza.

Lexi wasn't sure what else to say. She'd never been on a date before. Really, she hadn't been to a restaurant before without her family members. Friends weren't something she'd ever had.

"How has your day been so far?" Cameron asked her.

"Pretty good, as far as days go. I slept in a bit and snuggled with Daisy, then did some work." Lexi replied. She silently congratulated herself for being able to say she'd worked. She had a job now. She could say that. Maybe she wasn't a complete failure.

"What do you do for work?" Cameron asked as he grabbed a second slice of pizza.

Lexi blushed. "I actually just started, like yesterday," she admitted. "I was introduced to a lady who runs her own business and she's falling behind on some stuff. Hopefully I'll be able to help her. Right now, I'm going through receipts and entering them to keep track of expenses."

"Are you enjoying that? How many receipts do you have to enter?"

"I have no clue how many there actually are," Lexi replied with a laugh. "I'd guess a couple hundred, but that may be exaggerating. She gave me a shoebox full of them. And it's interesting, it's a job so I'll take it."

"How long will it take you to get a couple hundred receipts entered?"

"I have no clue," Lexi took a bite of pizza. "It depends on how many good days I have, how much time I'm able to spend doing computer work."

"Usable hours," Cameron replied, making Lexi give him a shocked look.

"Yes," She replied slowly. "That's a term I've used before." One that she usually used when talking to her support group or her doctors, but she didn't mention that.

"Is it rude if I ask about it?" Cameron's eyes didn't look at the cane. They didn't stray to the dog that Lexi had brought. They were focused on her. "I'm guessing the cane isn't a prop, and Daisy has a pretty good job."

Lexi blushed, surprised at the straightforwardness but not turned off by it. "I have POTS," she replied. "Postural Orthostatic Tachycardia Syndrome. It's a chronic..."

"Illness that affects your central nervous system." Cameron finished for her.

This time all Lexi could do was blink. She'd always had to explain what POTS was to people. The only ones who'd heard of it before were in her support group. She'd even had to explain it to various doctors before, or her mother had.

"I'm a nurse," Cameron explained at her questioning glance. "Not the most exciting of jobs, I know. But it was a lot less school and a lot less school loans than a doctor. Plus, I get paid pretty well. I've had a patient before with POTS, a couple years ago."

"I don't know what to say," Lexi admitted, taking a sip of her water. That small spark of attraction she'd felt when she met this man was growing by the moment. He hadn't run, he hadn't laughed. He'd actually heard of POTS, which wasn't common of most people she met.

Cameron shrugged. "I definitely don't know everything about it, probably not much at all. But I have heard of it before," he replied. He frowned as if he was trying to think. "It's usually something you are born with, or it comes with a traumatic illness or injury, from what I remember."

"When I was nine years old, I fell out of a tree and got a pretty bad concussion. My mom realized it was more than just your average concussion. So, after visiting a lot of doctors; a neurologist diagnosed me with POTS." Lexi shrugged. "I have a lot of different days, lots of migraines, all kinds of fun stuff. And I use a wheelchair a lot of the time. It saves me more energy."

"Daisy must be a big help," Cameron replied as he looked at the dog.

She thumped her tail when she heard her name. A dish of water sat next to her that neither Lexi nor Cameron had noticed the waitress bring.

"She's great," Lexi agreed.

"So now that we've talked about you, I should probably tell you all about the skeletons in my closet." Cameron changed the subject.

Lexi smiled and raised her eyebrows. "You have a lot of those?"

"Actually, I don't have any that I know of," Cameron shrugged one shoulder. "There's not much to know about me."

"I doubt that," Lexi grabbed a second slice of pizza. "Where did you grow up?"

"Grew up in Paris." Cameron replied, then took a bite of pizza before Lexi could question him.

She looked at him with a frown, wondering how that wasn't much to know. Paris wasn't interesting?

Cameron grinned. "Paris, Wisconsin," he explained with a chuckle. "It's in southeastern Wisconsin, part of Kenosha."

Lexi leaned back in her chair, her hand covering her mouth. "You really had me thinking you grew up in Europe," she said with a laugh.

"It would be interesting, but nope. Haven't actually been out of the States before. I'm not a fan of airplanes."

"You could go to Canada, there's no airplane required to go there."

"Well, I feel like that's cheating. It's attached to the States. Now if you were to go with me maybe I'd go..."

And just like that, conversation flowed as well as it had the first time they'd met.

Chapter 7

Lexi didn't note the time when she got home. It was late enough her parents had retired to their room. She tried to be as quiet as possible as she let Daisy out for a bathroom break and took her bedtime pills.

Once she made it to her room with Daisy, she took a breath. She'd dreamed of dates, but never imagined a perfect one. The one she'd had was as close as you could get. It had seemed more like a dream than reality. They'd finished the pizza, then walked a block away to sit by the lake and just talk for what had seemed like hours.

Lexi sat down in front of her floor length mirror. She took her earrings out and grabbed her hairbrush as she reminisced about the date. She'd learned that Cameron had no siblings, and had been raised by his aunt.

She grabbed a ponytail holder and pulled her hair into a low, loose ponytail to sleep in before changing into pajamas.

"What did you think of Cameron?" She asked Daisy.

Daisy lay on her bed and watched her, not making any moves to communicate.

Lexi frowned, watching the dog. "What's up?" She asked the dog. "Where was your tail wag? Or you could have growled if you didn't like him, I'd take that as an answer." She had a much different answer, but she didn't tell her dog that.

Daisy just stared at Lexi. Lexi's shoulders fell as she sat down on her bed next to Daisy.

"Is it my blood pressure?" She asked, reaching for her cuff. Lexi tried to relax as she put the cuff around her arm and started it. The excitement she still had from her date wasn't going to help it.

"Low-ish," she told Daisy after the device beeped. "You were waiting for it to get bad enough to alert me, weren't you?"

The dog watched as Lexi poured her packet of electrolytes into a water bottle and began to drink. She wasn't going to take her eyes off her owner for a while, that much she was making clear.

"Can I at least turn off the lights? That way I won't have to later when I'm tired." Lexi didn't give Daisy a chance to answer as she slid off her bed, literally, straight to the floor.

She'd tried to stand, but her vision had gone black. Going down to the floor was easier than trying to find her way around the room.

Lexi waited a minute until she could see again. This time she didn't bother standing. She crawled over to her Christmas lights and turned those on, then turned off her bedroom lights. She crawled back over to the bed and slowly climbed back on to it, leaning her back against the wall.

"Now I'm good," she told Daisy, who had been looking at her with judgment in her eyes.

Lexi sighed and drank the rest of her water. She grabbed her phone. She opened the chess app and began to play a game against the computer, quickly losing. She played again, this time making it a little bit longer before the computer defeated her as it always did.

She wasn't very good when pitted against a computer, but she could hold her own against other people. It helped to be able to read them. When she knew them, it was easier to predict their next move.

Speaking of... She thought as Rookie's username popped into her online friend list. She smiled and challenged him to a game.

You've been off chess for a whole day. I didn't know you could make it that long. Rookie had messaged her.

Lexi frowned. *I can play chess in real life too; it doesn't always have to be online. And maybe, just maybe, there are other things in life than chess.*

Other things in life? You're kidding.

Eating? Sleeping? Those are the basics at least.

You can't play chess in your sleep? Eating while playing chess is definitely possible.

Lexi couldn't hold back her giggle at that. *That's not what I meant.* She replied, wondering why she even tried.

It's so much more fun than what you meant.

Lexi shook her head as she took his queen. *You're off your game.*

Maybe I'm distracted.

Lexi didn't reply to that message. She chose to concentrate on the game instead. She was going to take advantage of his distraction. Or whatever he would claim it was next. A half hour later, she'd accomplished her goal and successfully put him in checkmate.

Congratulations Queen, Rookie typed. *I'm signing off, sweet dreams.*

Before Lexi could send anything in reply, she noticed that he was now offline. She smiled and closed the app. Maybe she would take that as her hint to go to bed herself.

"Kennel Daisy," she instructed her dog sleepily. "I want my bed back now."

***

"This isn't working." The man was faceless, but Lexi knew whose face it was supposed to be. "I can't handle this. I can't handle you. You are too much work and you'll never be able to do normal things like take a walk on the beach with me." The voice continued as the man looked at Lexi.

She could feel her body getting hot, as if she was burning up. She wanted to scream at him, to argue with him, but how could she? He was right. Of course, he was right. That was what she had said all along.

Lexi felt her cheeks dampen, then an extreme pressure on her chest. She fell to her knees and tried to breathe, but that became harder and harder...

Fur touched her cheeks, and Lexi took deep breaths as she opened her eyes. She was surprised to see darkness around her, and not the man she thought she'd been speaking to.

Daisy licked her cheek, trying to comfort her. Lexi realized that the sweating was real. She needed to lose some of these covers. And probably get a drink.

She glanced over to the nightstand, then remembered she had finished that last bottle of water with electrolytes a couple hours earlier. "Bring water Daisy," she told the dog, her voice hoarse.

The dog jumped off her legs and ran to the door, using her paw to open the handle. While she was gone, Lexi quickly peeled off layers of covers. She left only the sheet covering her. She was still hot, but she couldn't sleep unless something was over her.

Daisy brought the water bottle and gave it to Lexi, then pushed the door closed with her nose before she returned to her owner's side.

Lexi took a sip of water as she petted the dog, silently thanking her. She took another deep breath. It had only been a dream, that's why there was no face. Only a dream, nothing to think about.

She sighed softly as she put the water bottle on the nightstand and curled back up under her sheet. Daisy jumped off the bed and lay beside it, watching Lexi. She was ready to help if anything disturbed her person again.

And it did. Lexi had two more nightmares. One that involved a man leaving her behind as he went on a trip, and one that involved a man telling her she wasn't worth dating. Like the first, they had both featured a faceless man. After that third dream, Lexi checked her phone.

It was only 4am, still too early to get up. She could feel her a migraine coming, and a bit of dizziness too. Sleep felt hopeless at this point.

"I need sleep, sleep will help," she told Daisy. The dog had curled up on the bed beside her now that Lexi's night sweats had seemed to disappear. She was tired. Tired physically and tired emotionally by all these dreams.

"You're asleep, aren't you." Lexi sighed, rolling onto her back and looking up at the ceiling. She pulled a blanket on top of her, trying to get comfortable and fall asleep again. She tried to think about something else, maybe that would help her dreams.

Puppies, Lexi thought. *Puppies, how many breeds do I know? There's the Australian Shepherd, the Golden Retriever, the Bernese Mountain Dog, the Shetland Sheepdog, the...*

***

When Lexi woke up again, she quickly realized there was a problem.

Well - she amended - many problems. Her back was throbbing, as it did when she accidently fell asleep in the wrong position. Her head felt like it was so full of pressure it would soon explode. And worst of all, she had vertigo going full swing. Her room felt like it was spinning around her. Lexi knew if she tried to sit up, she would puke.

"Daisy," she groaned, wondering where the dog was. Last thing she remembered; Daisy had been asleep beside her.

Daisy's nose poked her cheek, as if she was checking on a patient. "What time is it?" Lexi asked her.

Daisy didn't reply. After all, that wasn't one of the skills she knew. A different day Lexi may have laughed at the idea of a dog being able to tell her the time; but today wasn't that day.

Lexi grimaced as she moved her arm, trying to find her phone. She was careful not to move her head. That would only send her into more spinning and a wave of nausea.

Lexi located her phone and brought it to her face, groaning at how much she spun when she tried to read the time. 8am, she noted thankfully, letting the phone fall onto her stomach. Sure, that hurt. But the pain would disappear in a moment.

"Daisy, get mom." Lexi instructed the dog. She heard the door open, and hoped that Daisy would be able to follow instructions. That wasn't a command they'd trained Daisy to perform. It was more a habit she had picked up. Hopefully in this instance it would be helpful.

Lexi closed her eyes. Instead of seeing darkness, she saw swirling blobs of color that were making her dizzier than ever. "Darn it," she said aloud, frustrated. No matter what she did, she'd be spinning.

There was no real way to fix it, at least not quickly. She had a pill to take, but that took a couple hours to kick in. A nap may help pass the time quicker, but not if there were hypnotic wheels on the back of her eyelids.

She heard footsteps in the doorway, louder than just Daisy's little paws. "Mom?" She asked.

"Daisy came and nudged me; she wouldn't leave until I followed her. What's wrong?" Connie asked her daughter. She put in her earring as she walked closer to the bed. She noted that the covers were all tangled together, something that had escaped Lexi completely.

"Vertigo," Lexi explained. "I need my pill, and my morning pills from the table." She frowned. "And I need to move to my side, because my back is not happy right now. But I'm afraid doing that will make me sick," she tried to hold back her tears as she spoke. She hated this feeling, this helplessness. Lexi liked taking care of herself. She hated when someone else had to help her.

Connie grabbed a pill box from Lexi's nightstand, then set it down again. "Why don't you try rolling over first? I'll go get a bucket in case, if you do get sick it won't do any good to have taken pills first. They will just come back up."

Lexi sighed, knowing her mom was right. "Okay," she agreed weakly.

"I'll be right back; I'm going to grab a bucket and your pills." Connie told her, patting a spot beside Lexi on the bed.

Daisy took her cue and jumped up. She lay down beside Lexi, laying her nose on Lexi's leg.

"Hey girl," Lexi told her, using her hand to pet the dog. Her fur was soft. Lexi tried to focus on that. A therapist she'd seen a couple years ago had said it was important to ground herself, to focus on things she could touch, smell, and see. Seeing was out of the question right now unless spinning rooms were helpful, so Lexi focused on touch.

"Okay hon," Connie walked back into the bedroom, then dropped some things on the floor. She grabbed a towel from the pile and lay it beside Lexi, on her bed. She handed Lexi a bucket. "Move slowly. It's okay if it takes you a while." Connie checked her watch.

Lexi clutched the bucket and tried to ignore the spinning as she carefully rolled to her side. She let out a sigh of relief when she made it, and gave the bucket back to her mom.

Connie set the bucket on her nightstand. "It will be here if you need it. Within reaching distance, but far enough from the edge you shouldn't be able to knock it over," she explained, then picked up the water bottle. "Do you want to sit to take your pills?"

"No, I'll just try to get my head up a little bit." Lexi said. She lay for a minute, then raised her head. She couldn't help the groan that came with the wave of nausea she felt.

Connie slipped another pillow under Lexi's head, helping her keep it up. "Your water bottle," she said as she pressed it into one of her daughter's hands. "It is already open. And here are your pills." She put those into Lexi's other hand.

Lexi slowly took the pills, feeling some relief as soon as she swallowed them. At least they would help eventually. She'd started the clock to being out of her vertigo prison.

Hopefully, sometimes it was bad enough the pill didn't work. Lexi didn't want to think about that.

Connie moved some of the covers that Lexi had tangled earlier, carefully putting each layer back onto Lexi.

"Drink this, it's one of your extra electrolyte beverages." Connie instructed as she took the water bottle back and screwed the lid back on. Lexi took a sip from the cup her mom had given her. She could tell which flavor it was from the smell of strawberries. It definitely had the salt of extra electrolytes. "Thanks Mom."

"You're welcome." Connie checked her watch. "The church service starts in five minutes; I am going to catch that online. If you need anything, send Daisy and I'll come." She set another bottle on Lexi's nightstand. "You have a bucket here, about half a water bottle still, and the rest of that electrolyte drink. I'll come see how you're doing after church is over in an hour and we can get you some food then."

Before Lexi could say anything, Connie was out the door and walking across the hall.

"Ugh Daisy," Lexi said before taking another sip of her drink. "I feel ugh."

She blinked then almost jumped at the nausea that sent through her. The hallway was full of light. It was a huge contrast to Lexi's dark room. "Daisy, close the door."

Daisy did as instructed, then came back and lay across Lexi's legs. Lexi tried to relax and let her body calm down, still sipping her electrolytes and petting Daisy.

***

Time passed; a lot slower than Lexi would have liked. The world was still spinning, and she was only getting more and more dizzy.

"Feeling any better?" Connie asked, walking into Lexi's room.

"No," Lexi groaned. "Worse."

Connie picked up Lexi's drink and inspected it. "You drank half of this, that's pretty good. Still spinning? The meds haven't kicked in yet?"

"I'd shake my head but that hurts. Everything hurts. Everything makes me dizzy," Lexi sighed. "I can't even close my eyes because there are spinning blobs on the back of them."

"I'm sorry honey," Connie smiled at her daughter, trying to calm her down. She pushed her hair out of her face. "Some of your hair, most of it actually, has escaped your ponytail. Would it help any if I fixed that for you?"

"I don't know," Lexi replied. Her mom was wearing a shirt Lexi guessed was striped, but seemed to be full of swirls when she looked at it. Anything she looked at spun around along with her bedroom.

Connie took the ponytail holder out of Lexi's hair. She pulled all of Lexi's hair together, then pulled it into a loose ponytail.

"Now, I know food is the last thing you want when you feel like this. But you do need some protein. What sounds the least yuck? Eggs? Peanut butter toast? A protein smoothie?"

Lexi grimaced and put her hand on her stomach. The thought of food made her insides churn. "Whatever is the least amount of eating," she told her mom.

Connie laughed. "That's understandable, I'll go grab one of those protein bars you like."

As she left the room, Lexi tried closing her eyes again. She opened them almost immediately; the blobs were still there.

"Daisy," she groaned. She hated this feeling, this helplessness that came over her sometimes. What good did having a job do right now? She couldn't move or sleep, working wasn't even a possibility.

Daisy put her nose into Lexi's back, then licked her cheek. "Thanks Daisy."

Connie brought Lexi a protein bar, then watched to make sure she ate it without any problems. "I need to get the grocery shopping done, so I will be gone for a while." She set a second protein bar on the nightstand. "Dad is home today, he will probably be watching tv in the living room all day."

"Thanks Mom," Lexi replied, trying not to let the light from the hallway hurt her eyes too much. "Close the door behind you please."

Connie did as asked and closed the door after leaving the room. After she left, Lexi found herself drifting off to sleep, the blobs on the back of her eyelids seeming to have gotten smaller.

***

Next thing Lexi knew, her mom was in her room again. She was holding a cup and a washcloth. "Any less dizzy?" Connie asked.

Lexi blinked slowly. "A little bit," she replied, mentally trying to figure out if she was any better. The room wasn't spinning, that fact was huge. She still felt dizzy and nauseous though.

"Yeah, a little better. The main spell is over, I think. I just have to recover." She tried not to think about how long that would take. Her longest spell had been a couple days. Hopefully this one would go away sooner.

"I have the rest of your drink here, it's cold. And I brought a cool washcloth for you to put over your eyes or your head, whichever would help you."

"My head," Lexi replied. She took the drink her mom offered and allowed her to set the washcloth in place. It did feel good, a welcome change.

"What time is it?" Lexi asked as she sipped on the drink.

Connie glanced at her watch. "3 pm. You missed lunch, but I thought the nap would probably be more helpful. Does food sound any better now?"

Lexi thought about it, realizing she was a lot hungrier now that the room had stopped spinning. "What is there to eat?"

"Shredded chicken sandwiches is what Dad and I had for dinner last night. There is some of that left over. I can just heat up the chicken and not put it on a bun if that's easier." Connie offered. She grabbed the blood pressure cuff and put it on Lexi's arm, then clicked the start button.

After the device beeped, Connie read the numbers. "Your blood pressure is in your average range. Keep eating and drinking your electrolytes, that would help."

"Okay. Did you feed Daisy? She needs to eat."

"She had lunch and breakfast," Connie confirmed. "I'll feed her dinner later too, I don't think you're going to make it out of your bed today. I'll go make you a sandwich."

Lexi watched her mom leave, then sighed. She didn't think so either, but it wasn't nice to hear from someone else.

Chapter 8

Lexi woke up the next morning feeling a lot closer to normal. Or normal for her, at least. The dizziness seemed to be gone, along with all traces of vertigo. The migraine remained, and Lexi felt like someone was taking a hammer to her head.

"I can move Daisy," Lexi announced as she sat up, head still pounding but not worsened. "Oh gosh, I forgot how amazing it is to be able to move."

That was the worst part of the vertigo for her. The being stuck in bed unable to do anything because any movement of her head made everything worse.

Daisy wagged her tail and walked over to sniff Lexi, as if she was checking for herself.

"I promise, I'm doing fine," Lexi told the dog and gave her a couple pets. Then she grabbed her meds and water bottle. She took her morning meds, along with her migraine pill.

I can move, Lexi thought again as she stood up and began to get dressed, *but moving is a lot slower than it should be. Hopefully I can kick this migraine and I'll be able to do my laundry today.*

A knock came at her door. "Lexi, how are you this morning?" Connie called.

"Better Mom," Lexi said as she pulled on her leggings. "Vertigo is gone, just a migraine."

"Good." Connie paused for a moment, and Lexi frowned as she pulled a sweatshirt over her head. Her mom was thinking, Lexi never knew what would come next.

"I made you breakfast. I'm going to catch my meeting if you're alright. I put Daisy's food in her bowl already, so you don't have to worry about that."

"Thanks Mom," Lexi replied as she pulled on her watch, then grabbed a pair of butterfly earrings and put those in. She sat down in the wheelchair that had strategically been left by her door.

She heard her mother's footsteps, then a door closing.

"Come on Daisy. Mom made both of us breakfast," Lexi said as she opened her door.

Daisy bolted out, down the hall in search of her food bowl. One would think she hadn't been fed for a week.

Lexi ventured into the kitchen and opened the fridge. She selected an iced coffee and opened it. She took a sip, then glanced over to the table to see what her mom had left for breakfast.

Oatmeal with strawberries from the looks of it. That wasn't the worst. Lexi strongly suspected her mom had snuck some protein powder into it, as Connie thought extra protein was the way to save the world.

By the time Lexi and her iced coffee made their way to the table, Daisy had already finished her kibble. She was outside as soon as Lexi opened the door.

Lexi ate her oatmeal slowly, enjoying being out of her room for the first time in twenty-four hours. Her head was still telling her she needed to take it easy today, but that was doable. Once she finished eating, Lexi put her dishes in the sink and made her way back to her room. She looked at her laptop longingly, wishing she could enter a couple more of those receipts.

Screens were never the answer to a migraine though. She would avoid that. She wasn't going to have a repeat of yesterday anytime soon if she could help it. She'd drank the coffee, hoping the caffeine would cure her migraine as it sometimes did.

Now Lexi was armed with two water bottles she intended to finish before lunch. "What should we do, Daisy?" She asked the dog. What could she do that wouldn't irritate her head more?

Usually, she would just take a nap or lay in her bed. But after yesterday that did not sound like the ideal choice. Laundry was an option, but Lexi still felt a little weak so she decided to try to tackle that later.

Daisy walked over to the closet, then came back over carrying a rope toy.

Lexi giggled. "That sounds like a great idea. I will absolutely play with you," she told the dog, scooting from her wheelchair to the floor. If she tried to play tug of war from her wheelchair it would just result in Daisy pulling her around.

"You're so strong," Lexi said as Daisy tugged on the other end of the rope, making soft growls as she played. "Such a tough puppy."

Lexi spent a lot of her day playing with Daisy. Her migraine never quite left. She had chess tomorrow and she didn't want to miss that. She did manage to finish her laundry, and she even took Daisy for a short "walk". Was it considered a walk if she was in a wheelchair? Either way, it had been good exercise for Daisy and good for both of them to get fresh air.

It was as Lexi was getting ready for bed that she realized she hadn't looked at her phone for almost forty-eight hours. It wasn't like she had any responsibility to her phone; Drew was really the only one to text her unless she was communicating with her parents.

She closed her eyes and relaxed for a moment, then grabbed the phone. Her curiosity was getting to her. She tapped the screen, noting that she had five notifications. Two were from her symptom journal, urging her to update her symptoms for the day. *At least yesterday's symptoms are easy to remember,* she thought as she opened the app and did as it urged.

Once she'd done that, she glanced at the other notifications. All three were from Cameron.

Lexi's shoulders fell as she realized she had completely forgotten about him. How had that happened? One part of her brain tried to argue that she'd been a little preoccupied. The other part was trying to convince her she was a terrible person.

Lexi opened the texts. Yesterday morning, he'd thanked her for a great date and told her again how much he'd enjoyed talking to her. He'd asked when he could see her again.

The second text came a couple hours later than the first, a response to one of the conversations they'd had on their date.

The third and final text had come an hour ago, apologizing for being so forward and saying he understood if she felt differently than he did.

Lexi bit her lip, hating that she hadn't thought to check her texts before now. This morning she could have spent five minutes on her phone. It wouldn't have irritated her head that much. But she had completely not thought about it. She looked at the messages again, unsure how exactly to respond.

Sensing she needed comfort; Daisy nudged her arm and laid her head across Lexi's lap.

"You're the best Daisy." Lexi whispered as she looked away from her phone for a moment. Her room was lit only by the Christmas lights, making her phone seem even more bright and ominous.

"Honesty is the best policy, right Daisy?" Lexi asked the dog, who was now fast asleep. "Lots of help you are."

She quickly typed out a reply. *I'm so sorry I did not reply to your messages sooner, I've been having a couple bad health days so I wasn't checking my phone. I'd enjoy going out with you again.*

Lexi sent that, then took a deep breath. She'd told the truth. How he reacted was on him. She set her phone down on the bed and ran her hands through Daisy's soft fur. The golden retriever snored a little bit as Lexi pet her, making Lexi giggle. "You have a problem," she told the dog.

Her phone buzzed beside her, and she grabbed it and checked the text immediately. *I understand, I should have thought about that possibility. Are you feeling better now?*

Lexi smiled. *Mostly, yes. I have a little bit of a lingering migraine but I can actually function now so that's a huge step in the right direction.*

Are you interested in doing something a little different for a date?

Lexi looked at her phone, trying to decipher the meaning of that. *Different?* She thought. *Different could mean a whole lot of things, what exactly was he suggesting?*

Her fingers flew as she typed back; *What do you mean by different?*

I mean a little earlier than we've had one before. I work a twelve-hour shift tomorrow, and I'd really rather not wait until Wednesday to see you again. Are you interested in a sunrise breakfast?

Lexi couldn't help the smile that came to her face. A sunrise breakfast sounded magical. Well, sort of. The early getting up did not sound that great. At least it would be for a good reason. And it wasn't that late, she could still get a decent amount of sleep.

That sounds like a great idea. What time and where?

Can we do 5:30am? If you'd rather wait till 6, we can do that too but the sun may have already risen. Where it is, is up to you. I have a brand-new deck in my backyard and a perfect view of the sunrise. But if you'd feel more comfortable meeting in a park, that works for me.

Lexi's eyes widened and Daisy raised her head as if she sensed an inner panic. "Daisy," Lexi whispered. "He's inviting me to his house, what the heck does that mean?" She looked at her phone again, rereading the text. That was what he was offering, and very politely. Lexi looked at Daisy as she tried to think.

Why not, her heart was screaming. She had Daisy. Daisy would not let anything bad happen to her.

I'll try to be awake that early. What is your address? She typed back before she could second-guess that decision. She blinked at the phone, suddenly wondering what she was supposed to tell her parents.

They'd notice she was gone when they woke up, and they'd worry. She had to tell them something. Maybe she'd leave a note before she left. If she texted, her mom would wake up in a worried panic. Connie always left her phone on at night in case Lexi needed her.

Lexi looked down at the phone in her hand when it vibrated, and her eyes widened in shock. *It's a couple blocks away from you – 934 Sundae Street.*

"Daisy," she breathed in shock.

She knew exactly where Cameron lived. She knew exactly what his house looked like. He was Drew's next-door neighbor.

Lexi gasped as the pieces of the puzzle started to come together. That was the reason he'd been at the block party. He'd said a neighbor had invited him – that had to have been Drew.

Daisy was watching her owner, trying to decide if she was worried or not. To tell the truth, Lexi wasn't sure herself what to think. She wondered if Cameron had put the pieces together. He knew she had a twin brother named Drew. But he knew nothing about Drew, she hadn't said anything about his house. And she and Drew looked nothing like twins. Lexi and Natala took after their dad, while Drew had gotten their mom's looks almost exactly. "Woah," she breathed again.

I look forward to seeing you tomorrow, goodnight. Cameron texted.

Lexi took a deep breath as she set alarms for tomorrow morning, then put her phone back on the nightstand. She was looking forward to tomorrow too, but she wasn't sure how she was going to fall asleep. Maybe she'd play chess for a while. When she opened the app, she was disappointed to find Rookie wasn't on.

Maybe playing with someone else will make me more tired, she thought as she clicked the button to join a random game.

***

Morning came way too early, but Lexi was wide awake. She'd tossed and turned all night, half in anticipation and nervousness.

She wasn't sure how much rest she'd actually gotten. Hopefully it was enough to enjoy her breakfast date and chess club this afternoon.

"I suppose I could take a nap this morning Daisy," Lexi said as she slowly stood up. The dog, laying in her kennel, seemed surprised that her master was awake so early this morning.

Daisy watched as Lexi got ready quietly. Lexi wished she could spray some perfume on, but she was so sensitive to smells it would give her a migraine in minutes.

"Daisy, come." Lexi called softly as she grabbed her cane and quietly opened her door. Daisy followed her to the bathroom where Lexi quickly brushed her teeth, trying to get rid of that morning breath. She left a note for her parents on the kitchen table, then grabbed her car keys and left the house.

Once Lexi closed the garage door behind herself, she felt like a weight had been lifted off her chest. She didn't need to tiptoe around anymore. It had been such a weird thing for her to do in the first place. *Makes me feel like I'm sneaking out,* Lexi thought as she opened the car door for Daisy.

Lexi was twenty-three, if she wanted to leave the house at any time she could. But she had never left without telling her mom where she was going at any time in the day. *Maybe it's past time I have,* she thought as she started her car.

The drive to Cameron's house was easy. She knew exactly where she was going and it wasn't far. As she pulled into Cameron's driveway, she couldn't help glancing over to Drew's house. There weren't any lights on, so he either was still asleep or wasn't home.

Lexi shook herself out of her thoughts as she got out of the car, then let Daisy out. By the time she had walked up the sidewalk, Cameron already had the front door open for her.

"Good morning," he greeted her. "It seems like a formal greeting, but it is early in the morning."

Lexi giggled. "It's earlier than I have been up for..." She trailed off as she tried to think, following Cameron through the house. "I don't actually know how long."

"I'm a little jealous of that, I'm up at sunrise almost every morning. Sometimes I'm at work after sunset." Cameron said as he opened a door that led to the backyard.

When Lexi stepped out, her gaze was drawn to the small table that was there. Breakfast had already been laid out – waffles and what looked like strawberry sauce. There was also an unlit candle sitting there, making it look a bit more romantic.

Cameron pulled out a chair. "M'lady," he said with a smile. "I hope you don't mind frozen waffles; I didn't have time to make them fresh."

"They smell delicious," Lexi said as she gestured for Daisy to lay down beside her.

Cameron grabbed a bowl of water that had been sitting on the table and set it down beside Daisy, then slid into the chair across from Lexi.

"That's the power of the microwave," he said. "Or maybe you smell the strawberry sauce, I did make that. My aunt taught me how, we always had it on special occasions with waffles."

"Is this a special occasion?" Lexi asked curiously as she took a waffle and added some strawberry sauce on top.

Cameron shrugged, looking a bit sheepish. "I'm not sure, but it seemed like it called for a special breakfast. I got out one of the candles my aunt keeps sending me, it's strawberry scented. I didn't light it though because I wasn't sure how sensitive you were to smells. I read yesterday that some people with POTS can be really sensitive to them."

Lexi paused, a bit of waffle halfway to her mouth. *He'd read about POTS?* "I can be, but it should be fine since we are outside. As long as it's not too intense of a scent."

Cameron looked at the candle. "I'll leave it how it is; I don't want to risk it," he replied. He watched as Lexi ate her first bite of her waffle. "Did I pick breakfast well?"

"I can't even tell they are frozen waffles; the strawberry sauce is so good," Lexi replied as she cut another bite. She glanced over at Drew's house.

"Did you know your neighbor is my brother?" She asked before putting the waffle in her mouth.

Cameron frowned and looked at Drew's house. "Drew is your brother? Your twin?" His surprise answered Lexi's question.

Lexi laughed. "Yes, he is. We don't look anything alike, do we?"

"You don't," Cameron replied, then backtracked for a moment. "I hope that's not offensive; I just wouldn't have guessed you were twins."

"Not offensive at all. Growing up people always thought our older sister and I were the twins. We look a lot more alike. It's a lot easier to see when Drew and I are together. We have some of the stereotypical twin things, like being able to communicate without words." Lexi took a bite of her waffle, hoping she wasn't rambling too much.

"That's not just a twin thing though, I think that can happen with any two people that are very close and know each other well enough," Cameron commented. "Do I need to watch my back now? Is he going to question me or tell me not to hurt his sister?"

Lexi blinked. "I don't know," she replied. "I've never dated before, so I don't have a clue how he would react. I haven't told him I'm dating either, so he may be surprised if he notices my car outside your house."

"You've never dated before?" Cameron asked, looking Lexi up and down. "And you're how old again, twenty-three?"

"Twenty-three." Lexi confirmed, gesturing to her cane. "I'm not exactly what guys consider a catch." She looked at him. "I'm guessing you have? Dated before, that is."

Cameron nodded as he took a bite of his waffle. He finished that before he explained. "I've been in two serious relationships before."

Lexi studied him, wondering if that was what this was. *What classified a relationship as serious? Did she want this to be a serious relationship?* Rather than ask Cameron either of those questions, she asked more about him. "Why did they end?"

"The first one I knew from high school. Really, we grew up together. When I chose to be a nurse instead of a doctor, she changed her mind about me." Cameron shrugged. "The second was just growing apart. We dated a couple years and it was more of a convenience than it was a connection. She met someone else and I wished her well. I actually went to her wedding last year."

Lexi considered that as she took a sip of her water. "That wasn't weird? To go to the wedding of someone you used to date?"

"It was weird, I can't argue that. But it wasn't awkward. There's a difference between the two, I've always thought." Cameron looked at the sky, which was now a beautiful orange as the sun began to rise. "These are my favorite days, when I get to stop and look at the sunrise. It's like the world is waking up."

Lexi followed his gaze. She had to agree, it was beautiful. There was something almost exclusive about being awake before the sun.

Topic turned to dogs as the pair finished their breakfast and watched the sun rise. It seemed only a couple minutes later that Lexi had to leave so Cameron could get ready for work.

"Enjoy your day," she told him as he held open the front door for her and Daisy.

"I'll try. I don't think the rest of it will be able to live up to the sunrise." Cameron told her.

Lexi blushed as she walked down the sidewalk. She opened the car door for Daisy, looking toward Drew's house as she did. He was getting into his car, likely to go to work. She looked away, wondering if he'd noticed her car or not.

Oh well, it wasn't like it was a secret that she was here. If Drew asked, she'd tell him the truth. And if he didn't ask, then he probably hadn't seen her.

"Okay Daisy, let's go home," Lexi told her dog. "Maybe we can get some receipts entered before we eat lunch and go to the chess club. I feel like I have energy and I want to take advantage of it."

Chapter 9

Lexi did take advantage of that energy, which was more adrenaline than anything. She went home and worked on the receipts for a couple hours. She tried to keep up with her water and electrolytes as she ate lunch, then ran to the chess club. But as she left the library, she could feel that her body wasn't working how it should.

Daisy could tell too. A fact made evident as she whined all the way home. She was still whining as Lexi wheeled into the house, something Connie noted immediately.

"What have you done today?" She asked, before disappearing into Lexi's room to grab her blood pressure monitor.

"Hello to you too," Lexi muttered as she made her way to the table and set down her empty water bottle. "Yes, the chess club went fine. Thank you for asking," she buried her hands in Daisy's fur as the dog nudged her.

Connie grabbed Lexi's arm and strapped on the blood pressure monitor, then clicked the button to start it before she went to the fridge. She took one of Lexi's rapid rehydration drinks and set it on the table the same moment the monitor beeped.

"Alexica Luna," Connie scolded her. "You're seventy-one over thirty-nine. That's pretty low, how didn't you notice this?"

"Mom, I'm an adult. You don't have to scold me," Lexi sighed as she opened the bottle and started to down the drink.

"Do you need some food? I can get one of your protein bars."

"I'm fine. Well, not fine but I can do stuff myself. I'm just low and lightheaded. There's no vertigo. I can move," Lexi told her mom. She had done too much today and she'd known it. But she had felt happy. She felt like she could accomplish something, and wanted to try.

Now she was paying the price, she mused as she and Daisy went to their bedroom. "I'm sorry for not listening to your alert Daisy, you did a good job. Good girl, good alert." Lexi halfheartedly praised the dog. She hoped Daisy understood that she did a good job. The disappointment in Lexi's voice was directed at herself.

She glanced at her computer, wishing she could pick up where she had left off earlier with the receipts. It would be simple work; it shouldn't take too much of her energy.

Daisy eyed Lexi as if she was crazy, making Lexi sigh. "I know girl, don't do it. My body has had enough and I need to stop," she petted the dog, trying to calm down. Her brain seemed scrambled. The anxiety was starting to seep in.

"I should try to take a nap." Her shoulders fell as she looked at her bed, knowing that would be the smart thing to do. It wasn't what she wanted to do. But when she started a flare what she wanted to do was no longer relevant.

***

When Lexi woke up to Daisy's nudging, she realized it was dark out. "Why? How is it dark already?" She muttered, sitting up. She must have tried doing that too fast because as soon as she did her vision went black. "Daisy, get me water please."

The dog returned with the water, and Lexi praised her before taking a drink. She picked up her phone. It was already close to 9pm. She thought back to when she'd fallen asleep, her head throbbing.

"I missed a pill," she told Daisy. "I should have taken one when I got home from chess but I completely forgot, now I'm going to pay for that."

She looked around her room, wondering why her mom hadn't woken her up to eat dinner. Apparently Lexi had seemed so bad when she got home that Connie had thought she needed sleep.

Lexi slowly got up and moved to her wheelchair, then made her way to the kitchen. "Hey honey, how are you feeling?" David asked when he noticed her.

"Not great," Lexi replied as she opened the fridge. She tried to ignore her head as she pulled out a container. She stood for a moment to grab a plate, then took both to the table. She couldn't stand long enough to move the portion of chicken she would eat from the container to the plate. It seemed so stupid; she'd been using her cane this morning.

That may also have something to do with this, Lexi thought as she put her food in the microwave.

David made his way to the kitchen and put the container back away for Lexi, and got her food out of the microwave for her.

"Thanks," Lexi told him grudgingly, taking her food to the table. She opened her container of pills and pulled out her bedtime one to take with her dinner.

"I guess I'll be awake late tonight, if I'm eating now." Lexi told her dad before stabbing her fork into a piece of chicken.

"Good thing you got such a long nap." David replied lightheartedly as he grabbed a box of cereal and filled a bowl. "I fed Daisy for you; she ate at five like normal." He added milk to the bowl and grabbed a spoon, then sat down at the table across from Lexi.

"So, you left a note this morning about going to a boy's house. This something I should be worried about?"

Lexi stared at her dad, unsure what to say to that. "What do you want to know? He was at that picnic; you probably saw him there. Drew knows him I guess, they are neighbors."

David considered this, watching his daughter. "He knows about your stuff?"

Lexi raised her eyebrows as she ate a bite of potato. "My POTS?" She asked. "Yeah, he's seen it before. He's a nurse," she added as an explanation.

David shrugged. "Sounds like that would be good for you."

"That's it?" Lexi asked, picking up another potato with her fork. "You're fine with me going to his house and whatever?"

David shrugged. "Don't see what I should be worried about. If he breaks your heart I'll be here, but you're smart. You know all the lines Drew likes to use, so you know to avoid all that smooth talk."

Lexi laughed, ignoring the pain that brought to her head. "That's true," she replied. "Is he dating anyone at the moment? I haven't heard of anyone since that last girl that looked like barbie."

David shrugged. "Not sure. Monica, I think, was her name. I don't keep up with all that stuff. That's your mom's job."

Lexi smiled as she took her pill, then ate the last bite of her dinner. That seemed about right. "Goodnight Dad," she called as she made her way to her room.

"Goodnight youngest daughter of mine," David called back.

Lexi closed her bedroom door and looked at her dog. "Are you going to get mad at me if I use the computer?" She asked Daisy, who was still eyeing her. "I need to do something. I can't go to sleep for another two or three hours."

Daisy nudged her, making Lexi's shoulders fall. "I'm still low?" She asked, not really needing confirmation. The dog was smart. She knew Lexi was low.

Lexi grabbed an electrolyte packet and added that to her half-empty water bottle. She winced a bit as she took a sip. The salt was strong. *It's because of that missed pill,* she thought. *Why the heck did I not think to take that? I could have woken up feeling decent.*

She took a deep breath and finished the water, realizing she should have grabbed another bottle while she was in the kitchen. *Oh well, I can send Daisy for another one later.*

Lexi carefully grabbed her pajamas, then attempted to get changed. It was made harder by the fact that she couldn't stand without feeling like she was going to pass out, so she was trying to dress while still in her wheelchair. It was a lot harder than it sounded, and was taking more energy than she knew she had.

After she changed, she grabbed her phone and checked to see if she'd had any messages while she slept. There was one from her mom, telling her she was going to bed and hoped that Lexi's nap would help her. There was also one from Cameron that said he'd enjoyed the sunrise, and asked when they could do it again.

Lexi looked around her room, thinking through her day. It had been a great morning. She'd gotten some work done, been able to make chess club... then she'd just slept for hours. It seemed more like the routine of a seventy-year-old than a twenty-three-year-old. It shouldn't be the routine of a twenty-three-year-old. But that was the hand Lexi had been dealt.

Lexi felt tears come to her eyes. How could she put someone else through this life of hers? What had she been thinking, trying to date someone?

Cameron was thirty. He worked twelve-hour shifts at the hospital and could still make breakfast before that. He'd get tired of her and all her health problems soon enough.

Lexi couldn't ask someone to make plans with her that she may cancel at the last second because she started to feel awful. She couldn't ask anyone to help her all the times she needed it but didn't want to admit that. Sure, Daisy was a great help, but she couldn't do everything.

And hey, Lexi was making some of her own money now, but that may be a temporary thing. Even if it wasn't, she'd never make enough to support herself and Daisy.

How could she ask someone else to take that on? She was simply a burden. For her parents, for Drew growing up; how could she ask someone else to shoulder that?

Lexi didn't even realize the tears were coming down in steady streams now. She hugged Daisy, who had run to her aid as soon as she began crying. "I have you, Daisy. I don't deserve that, much less an actual human. What could I do for anyone?"

Lexi didn't even remember sending a text in reply. She didn't remember the hours she spent crying that night, and didn't remember the endless hugs she'd given Daisy.

When she woke up in the morning – on her bedroom floor – it all seemed like a blur. And worse, she felt so weak she couldn't move. "Daisy, get Mom," she told the dog quietly, hating the fact that she couldn't get up from the floor by herself.

Chapter 10

It was twenty-four hours later – on Thursday morning – that Lexi finally emerged from her room again. She'd be the first to admit that she looked like a mess. Her hair was tangled and it was evident she'd been crying.

"You look absolutely awful." A voice came from the table.

Lexi blinked, then frowned when she saw her sister. "What are you doing here?" She asked, opening the fridge to grab a yogurt cup. She should have been more polite. She should have been excited to see Natala, but at the moment she was tired.

"I moved in," Natala shrugged. "Well, for a week or two at least. I'll be moving into an apartment at the end of the month but for now here I am."

"Why didn't anyone tell me?" Lexi asked as she opened her yogurt and stabbed it with a spoon. She was perturbed no one had thought to tell her Natala was actually moving in. She lived in this house too.

Why was everything happening so quickly? She wasn't prepared.

Daisy nudged her, and she glanced at the dog. "Food," Lexi said aloud as she wheeled over to fill the golden retriever's bowl. "Sorry Daisy."

"I just told Mom I was coming Tuesday, and from the sounds of it you weren't doing well so she didn't tell you." Natala explained, dipping her spoon into her own yogurt. "Back to my original statement, why do you look like your dog died? She's sitting right there eating so I know that's not what happened."

Lexi took a bite of her yogurt, wondering if she even wanted to get into this with her sister. Natala had left years ago. She probably didn't remember what a day was like for Lexi. She'd never experienced it herself. How would she be able to understand?

"Because life," Lexi replied, not meeting her sister's gaze. It wasn't worth going into. Lexi should just finish her breakfast and get back to her room.

Natala watched her without blinking. "Does it have to do with the kid who was here yesterday asking for you?" She frowned. "Okay, that sounds weird. I'm pretty sure he's older than I am. Which also seems weird. You're dating someone older than I am."

"Not dating," Lexi replied as she tried to ignore Natala's words. One statement in particular had caught her attention. "What do you mean he was here yesterday?"

"Maybe being older is a good thing. He'd be mature, have a better understanding of life. You've always had an old soul," Natala continued as if she hadn't heard Lexi. "Plus, you need someone mature. You don't have time or energy for the games some men play."

"Natala," Lexi waited until her sister looked at her. "What do you mean, someone was here yesterday?"

"Guy named Cameron?" Natala shrugged. "He came by yesterday, saying he'd gotten the address from Drew and needed to talk to you. You sent a text or something. Drew didn't know you were dating, but Dad did and he explained."

"I can't date," Lexi replied offhandedly, wondering why Cameron had come to her house.

She'd texted him something Tuesday. She couldn't quite remember what. Something to the effect of "I'm done", probably some of the cliché "it's me, not you" too.

Natala laughed, covering her mouth with her hand. "That's funny. You can't date. Gosh Lexi, you're not a robot or anything. Anyone can date."

"Very nice Natala. I know anyone can date, but there's no point. I'm not normal, I'm not worth it and I'm a lot of work."

Natala set down her spoon. "Who told you that you aren't worth it? Seriously, point them out and I will be happy to set them straight.

You have a chronic illness. You're not dying or anything. You're a person and you are plenty worth it."

Lexi shrugged. "No one had to tell me that. It's pretty easy to figure out. I'll never be able-bodied or helpful to anyone. I'll never be able to work enough to support myself or Daisy. I couldn't make it on my own. How am I supposed to rely on someone else to take care of me? To take on the burden of caring for me on days like yesterday and last week when I can't get out of bed?"

"Alexica," Natala took a breath, trying to figure out how to reach her sister. "You aren't a burden. I doubt mom or dad would ever call you that. I know Drew wouldn't. Heck, I always felt left out because everyone ran to do whatever you needed. If someone cares about you, they will be happy to help you. Happy to take care of you when you need it. They will try to understand you." She looked her younger sister in the eyes.

"You act so obsessed with yourself sometimes. It's all about what you can do or what you can't do. What about other people? What if other people want to help you? What if you bring value to someone else?"

Lexi stared at her sister. She wasn't self-obsessed, she was broken. There was a big difference there. "I'm not self-obsessed," she protested.

Natala stood up. "It's all about you, every sentence you told me about not dating was 'I'. Did you actually talk to the guy? Did you explain your challenges to him, ask if he's still interested? Dad said he's a nurse. I'd imagine he'd be pretty decent at taking care of people and maybe willing to learn a thing or two about all your issues. You are really great at feeling bad for yourself, playing the victim. I get that you aren't the same as everyone else. You have limitations, you have prescriptions, whatever. That doesn't mean you're broken. That doesn't mean it's all about you and your problems." Natala walked down the hallway, effectively ending the conversation.

Lexi looked at Daisy, unsure what to even think. Did she do that? She couldn't actually do that, she wasn't self-obsessed. "Am I, Daisy?"

She tried to think back to the past week, trying to figure out if there was anything true in what Natala was saying. She did feel sorry for herself a lot, that part she couldn't argue. When she couldn't move there wasn't much else to think about. But obsessed seemed like it was going a little far.

Lexi tried to go about the motions of her day, as much as she could at least. She was careful to only spend an hour working on the receipt pile. She drank some extra electrolytes before the chess club, and made sure to bring her pills with her so she couldn't forget to take the one after the chess club.

***

"Lexi, you look less pale today." Patsy greeted her with a hug as she walked into the room a half hour early.

Lexi smiled. "Thanks, I feel better today than I did Tuesday. I wasn't watching myself as much as I should have been."

"I'm glad you are doing better. We will have a new helper today; you'll have to show him the ropes a bit. You should know them well enough." Patsy winked at her as she set down the bins. "I'll be back. I have to help at the desk for a little bit yet. We had two story times today, so breaks have been a little weird." She left the room, and Lexi opened the top bin.

She'd set up for the club by herself before. It wasn't as much fun as having Patsy help, but she was perfectly capable.

Lexi put as many of the chess mats as she could fit on her lap, then rolled over to the first table. She pulled the rubber band off one of the mats and set it on the table.

"Lexi?"

Lexi looked up, surprised to see Cameron here. Why was he at the library? In the children's section, no less.

"I'm here to help with the chess club. The librarian at the desk said to come in and someone would tell me what to do." Cameron explained, putting his hands in his pockets.

Lexi paused, still surprised that he was there. "You play chess?" She asked finally as she moved to the next table and unrolled that mat.

"I'm not an expert, but I know how."

Lexi eyed him, wondering how that had never come up in the conversations they'd had. They had talked about many things but chess was never one of them. She sighed inwardly. He was here and no matter what her current feelings were, more help would make set-up go faster.

"In the bottom bin, there are canvas bags with the pieces in them. If you want to start setting those up that would be great," she told him before continuing to the next tables.

Cameron walked over to the bins. He moved the top one aside, then opened the bottom one. He pulled out a couple canvas bags, then sat down at the first table Lexi had set a mat at.

Lexi tried to watch as he set up the pieces, half wondering if he'd be able to set them up right. If you didn't know chess well, it was easy to mess up. The knights and bishops were easy to mix up positions, as well as the king and the queen.

"I know how to set up a chess board," Cameron said softly as he caught her glancing over.

Lexi blushed, moving on to a table so her back was to him. "Just wanted to make sure," she replied. "Sometimes we have the kids do it, so they learn how. But it takes them a little while and the chess club only lasts an hour and a half."

She finished setting up the chess mats, and grabbed a couple canvas bags for herself. Daisy was watching her carefully from the corner. "I'm fine Daisy," she told the dog as she passed her.

Daisy's tail thumped against the wall, making Lexi smile. She began to set up one of the tables silently. She wasn't sure what she would even have said to Cameron, so she chose silence.

"Okay, the desk is covered." Patsy walked into the room and looked around. "It looks like you've gotten a great start here. Lexi, you met Cameron?"

"We've met." Lexi tried to keep her voice even, but Pasty knew her well enough to give her a look.

"Wonderful," Patsy replied, a large smile on her face. "The kiddos will be here in ten minutes. Lexi, Chelsea's mom called this morning to tell me Chelsea will be coming again. Do you want to play with her today, and Cameron and I can walk around?"

"Sure," Lexi replied. Chelsea was a first-grader who had come last week for the first time. She'd never played chess, knew nothing about the game. Last week Lexi had tried to teach her as she helped a couple other pairs, but that hadn't worked the best. It would be easier to explain with her as they went; which she could do this week because they had extra help.

Lexi continued to set up chess pieces until the first of the kids began to come in. Then she sat back and waited for Chelsea.

***

"Well, I'd call that a successful day. A record day I think," Patsy said an hour and a half later after all the kids had left.

Lexi smiled. "I'm not sure. That one week when I was younger there were like thirty of us," she replied as she took a sip of water.

"There were only twenty, I think. It just seemed like a lot more because you were a lot smaller." Patsy replied.

Lexi frowned as she began to put away the pieces that she and Chelsea had been using. "I'm not sure about that. I swear I remember you calling it a record week."

"Patsy, can you help this young lady find a book about dinosaurs?" Another librarian asked, standing in the doorway with a little girl.

"Sure! I know exactly where the dinosaur books are, we have a lot of them," Patsy said as she followed the girl out of the room.

Lexi smiled, remembering when she had been a girl like that. Always asking for help finding books on topics that interested her at the time. Reading had been easy for her to do, something that didn't require much physical energy to keep her entertained.

"You've been part of this for a while then?" Cameron asked her as he began to pick up the pieces at a table beside her.

"Since I was eleven," Lexi answered. "It was something to do, and then it became fun and I guess I liked it so much I never left." She shrugged as she dropped the canvas bag onto her lap and moved on to the next table. "Not like I have too many other things to do with my time. This has always been a good use of it."

"I stopped by your house yesterday," Cameron said, watching her.

"I know." Lexi didn't meet his gaze. "Natala - my older sister - told me about that as she was yelling at me this morning. She told me I was self-obsessed."

Cameron raised his eyebrows. "Do I just put this back into the tote?" He asked.

Lexi nodded, watching as he did so. "She might be a little right," she admitted. "I do think of myself quite a bit. In my defense – not that I deserve it – I spend way too much time alone in my thoughts."

"Do you remember how I said in my last serious relationship that there was no connection?' Cameron asked her, sitting down at the table across from her.

Lexi looked him in the eye this time. "Yes."

"I felt a connection with you. I feel a connection with you," Cameron told her as he laid one of his hands on hers, stopping her from cleaning up the pieces.

There was a chess piece clenched in the middle of her hand, something Cameron didn't seem to realize.

"I have never been able to talk to someone for hours. I've heard that expression but I never understood what it meant. Or believed it was possible, until I spoke to you at that picnic."

Lexi blinked, looking at their hands. "I'm broken," she said, trying not to let any tears escape. "I'm not like any of the girls you've dated before. I spent two of the past seven days unable to get out of bed. I can't get up and watch the sunset every morning. I'll never be able to support myself," she glanced over at her dog. "Or Daisy. And maybe my sister had a little bit of a point when she told me I think about myself too much."

"I'm a nurse, Lexi. That doesn't make me a saint by any means. But it does mean I know how to take care of people. It's one of my favorite things to do. I watched my aunt step up and take care of me when she shouldn't have had to. I've made it my mission to take care of other people as a way to repay that kindness. I'm not perfect, I spend long shifts at the hospital and sometimes they aren't easy days."

Cameron reached out and tipped Lexi's chin up so she was looking him in the eye again. "And Lexi, I'd spend any sunrise with you if I could. No matter where that is or what it looks like. If you can't get out of bed, I'd try to be right beside you."

Lexi felt a smile creep across her face. "I've never been in a relationship before. I don't know how any of this works," she admitted. "And I'm not sure I'd be any good at it. But I really like talking to you, and you make me smile a lot."

"You make me smile a lot too. And I like being around you, no matter what that looks like. Dating and relationships look different for everyone. We can make it work for us. I just want to spend as much time with you as I can, spend any sunrise with you that I'm able. And Daisy, because I know she goes where you go. I'd be happy to spend time with your family too, because I know you spend a lot of time with them."

Lexi felt like she was melting inside a bit. "Okay," she whispered.

"Okay?" Cameron repeated, excitement in his voice.

Lexi gave him a big smile. "Okay," she repeated, looking down at her hand as she felt a prick. "You've trapped a piece in my hand." She pointed out.

Cameron lifted his hand off hers, something she was surprised to find that she missed almost immediately. She opened her hand and set the rook that had been trapped in it on the table.

"That's my favorite chess piece. I even used it in my username for the online chess app thing I have. I'll love the rook for life," Cameron commented.

Lexi felt her heart skip a beat. She almost forgot to breathe as she processed that statement. *It couldn't be, could it? That would be insane.* But she had to know.

"Rookieforlife?" She asked in a whisper.

Cameron frowned. "Yes," he replied. "How did you know that?"

"My username is QueenLuna," Lexi replied.

Cameron blinked, then grinned at her in wonder. "Maybe there was a reason we clicked. We'd already known each other for years. Just when I thought you couldn't get any more perfect."

Lexi blushed and looked at the floor. Cameron took her hands both in his. "Can I kiss you?" He asked softly.

Lexi felt her cheeks go red. "Sure."

That was the first time Patsy caught them kissing in the classroom, but it wouldn't be the last. They had a lifetime of talking, playing chess, and kissing to do between watching any sunrise they could together.

Did you love *Any Sunrise*? Then you should read *Italian Sunsets* by Kimberly R. Rose!

Natala Luna always wanted to travel. In her dreams, she never imagined she'd be doing it solo. However, after ending a ten-year relationship, she finds herself headed to Italy. She cannot wait to indulge in the food and see the sights.

As for romance, the only thing she's interested in falling in love with is gelato.

But is it fate that she meets Tony Calo on the plane? The handsome travel photographer seems to show up everywhere she goes. When he asks Natala to watch the sunsets with him, she can't help but feel the magic. But will the Italian sunsets be enough for Natala to fall in love again?

Also by Kimberly R. Rose

Luna Family Trilogy
Italian Sunsets
Italian Sunsets
Any Sunrise

About the Author

An early childhood educator turned small business woman and author; Kimberly R. Rose grew up in a small town in Wisconsin. She has loved reading since she was a child, often neglecting her schoolwork to read a book. That love for reading turned into inspiration for writing. Her favorite things in life are her faith, her family, and chocolate.

Italian Sunsets is Kimberly's debut novella, the first in the Luna Family Trilogy.